from the inkhorn & plume of

JULIANNA BAGGOTT

a yearling book

Text copyright © 2009 by Julianna Baggott
Cover and interior illustrations copyright © 2009 by Brandon Dorman

All rights reserved. Published in the United States by Yearling, an imprint of Random House Children's Books, a division of Random House, Inc., New York. Originally published in hardcover in the United States by Delacorte Press, an imprint of Random House Children's Books, a division of Random House, Inc., New York, in 2009.

Yearling and the jumping horse design are registered trademarks of Random House, Inc.

Visit us on the Web! www.randomhouse.com/kids

Educators and librarians, for a variety of teaching tools, visit us at www.randomhouse.com/teachers

The Library of Congress has cataloged the hardcover edition of this work as follows:
Baggott, Julianna.
The Ever Breath / Julianna Baggott. — 1st ed.
p. cm.
Summary: Twins Truman and Camille, spending winter break with their parental grandmother, follow a secret passageway to the Breath World, where creatures of magic dwell, to find the Ever Breath, a magical stone that maintains balance between worlds.
ISBN 978-0-385-73761-6 (hardcover) — ISBN 978-0-385-90676-0 (lib. bdg.)
ISBN 978-0-375-89368-1 (ebook)
[1. Space and time—Fiction. 2. Magic—Fiction. 3. Twins—Fiction. 4. Brothers and sisters—Fiction. 5. Missing persons—Fiction.] I. Title.
PZ7.B14026Eve 2009
[Fic]—dc22
2009001359

ISBN 978-0-375-85114-8 (pbk.)

Printed in the United States of America

10 9 8 7 6 5 4 3 2 1

First Yearling Edition 2011

Random House Children's Books supports the First Amendment and celebrates the right to read.

This book is dedicated to those inhabitants of the Fixed World
who have led me to the Breath World and back again—
Glenda, Bill, Phoebe, Finneas, Theo, Otis, and Dave.

And thank you, Wendy, Nat, and Justin,
for tending the passageway.

The universe is made of stories, not atoms.
—Muriel Rukeyser

CHAPTER ONE

Swallow Road

It was cold outside, and the car's heater smelled like a wet dog—even though they didn't have a dog. Truman Cragmeal had always wanted one, but he was allergic to fur—well, to pet dander, actually.

Truman was allergic to a lot of things. Strawberries made him break out in itchy hives. Nuts made his throat tighten. Bee stings caused him to swell up all over. Chocolate gave him a headache. Pollen clogged his nose. He was lactose intolerant and mildly asthmatic. He carried an inhaler in one front pocket of his pants and an EpiPen, in case of severe allergic reactions, in the other at all times.

Worst of all for Truman at this very moment was the fact that he easily became carsick and his mother was driving along back roads that curved and twisted, dipping in and out of a misty fog.

To take his mind off his carsickness, Truman was trying to concentrate on the dog he'd never have. With his stomach full of belchy air, he decided on a Chinese fighting dog— the kind with all the extra skin and the smushed, wrinkly face. He closed his eyes and pictured the Chinese fighting dog but, in his imagination, the dog quickly sprouted horns and then wings and then webbed claws. Truman's brain always seemed to play tricks like that. It was the kind of thing that made his mind wander in class and got him in trouble with his teacher, Ms. Quillum.

He burped and opened his eyes. He thought it'd be good to have a dog, especially now that his dad was gone. *Boys need dogs*, he thought, even though he knew he'd never be allowed to have one and wouldn't be able to breathe if he did.

Truman's twin sister, Camille, was sitting next to him. She was reading a book about someone who'd climbed a mountain and almost died and ended up having to have his nose amputated because of frostbite.

One month earlier, before their father left, Camille had been a girl who wore pink Girl Power sweatshirts and wrote her homework in sparkle gel pens and dotted her *i*'s with hearts.

But now she wore black T-shirts and camouflage pants and spent her spare time watching TV shows where people were dropped off in the middle of the jungle with only a piece of flint, and reading books on disasters—plane crashes, circus fires, shipwrecks, tsunamis, earthquakes, floods. She tied back her curly dark hair with leather shoelaces and sometimes insisted on eating without silverware.

She never got carsick, and unlike Truman, she wasn't lactose intolerant, never got hives, and didn't swell up when stung by a bee. She wasn't allergic to pet dander or pollen. She didn't need an inhaler. She didn't even wear glasses. Truman's glasses had thick lenses that weighed them down, and he always had to keep pushing them back up the bridge of his small nose. Truman didn't understand how he and Camille could be twins. They were complete opposites.

The car crested a small hill and Truman's stomach flipped and he moaned a little.

"Really, Truman," Camille said. "Please don't barf."

"I don't barf on purpose, you know!"

"This is the right way, don't you think?" Truman's mother said nervously. She was sitting right on the edge of the seat, in close to the wheel, squinting through the windshield. She'd forgotten the map, as well as the directions and her glasses. Since their father left, she'd had to work harder and harder, taking on an extra job at night where she answered phones for doctors who were on call but were at the opera or something. She worked so hard that she forgot things. She was dropping Camille and Truman at their grandmother's so that she could work extra hours over the holidays and get paid overtime. Truman wondered whether she might work so hard over the holidays that she'd forget to come back for him and Camille. He knew it wasn't logical—his mother would never forget them—but still the idea worried him a bit. "Swallow Road? Is that what we're looking for? Like the little bird, the swallow?" his mother asked.

It was a strange name for a road, and Truman remembered it distinctly. "That's what you said before," he told her. "Swallow Road. It seems like the kind of road that could get *swallowed* up." There were only a few houses and bare trees and lots of cloud-clotted sky. Truman felt the hot itch of panic in his chest. He was afraid now that the car trip might go on forever. What if they never found the place?

"A road being swallowed?" Camille said. "It's named after the bird. Trust me."

"Did I say left or right?" his mother asked.

"Are we *still* lost?" Camille asked.

"We're not lost," their mother said. "Just misplaced."

"Ah, right, *misplaced*," Camille said. "Like Dad, I guess. He isn't lost. He's just *misplaced?*"

Camille was fearless about bringing up their father. Every time she did, Truman started breathing heavily, as if he were going to have an asthma attack, just to distract everyone, which was what he did now. He began a wheezy inhale, but Camille glared at him.

"Stop faking."

Truman stopped midbreath. He was a little scared of Camille these days.

"Your father isn't lost *or* misplaced," his mother said. "He's just been called away on business."

"He's a manager of three Taco Grills," Camille said flatly. "Has he been called in to Taco Grill headquarters? Is he a Taco Grill *spy* now?"

"Stop it," his mother said. "Just have a little faith in him. That's all I ask." And she sighed with deep exhaustion. She sometimes reminded Truman of a rowboat without oars, drifting out across a lake. She used to have lots of energy, and she'd been the type to charge around with purpose and wear lipstick and brush her hair, but now her lips were pale and she pulled her hair back in a tangled ponytail and she seemed to shuffle and drift, usually forgetting to take her name tag off, and so there was a plastic badge pinned to her shirt that read "Hello. My Name is Peggy Cragmeal. May I help you?"

Sometimes Truman could pretend that his father was still living with them and was just out picking up something at the dry cleaner or making a grocery-store run. But then he would look at his mother's tired eyes or at Camille wearing her camouflage backpack and he couldn't pretend anymore. He sometimes wondered if *he'd* changed, but he didn't think he had.

"Must be a nice house to be on a golf course!" Truman said brightly. Their grandmother's house supposedly had a view of the seventeenth hole at a ritzy club, and Truman was trying to change the mood a little. His teacher, Ms. Quillum, often said, "Happiness is contagious!" She smiled when she said this, an enormous smile that took up most of her small round face.

"I'm sure it will be a lot of fun," his mother said. She didn't sound convincing.

And then, as if by sheer luck, Truman saw a sign for the Gilded Capital Country Club. His mother had passed it. "There it is!" he shouted, twisting around in his seat. "Back there!"

It was almost dusk as they rolled under the wrought-iron entranceway that spelled out *GCCC* in gold cursive. They followed a road past the clubhouse to the edge of the nearly empty parking lot. Truman's mother parked the car and turned off the engine. The heater let out one last puff of dogginess and the car went quiet, except for a few exhausted knocks of the engine.

Truman and Camille leaned forward between the bucket seats. Their mother rested her arms on the wheel. They looked down the sloping green of the fairway and saw a house—tall, ancient, with a rusty tin roof and boarded-up windows. It wasn't sitting on a road *beside* the golf course, as Truman had expected; it was actually sitting *on* the golf course itself—on the small hill of the seventeenth hole—all alone. On one side there was a sand trap, on the other side a pond, and right in front of it the green, and stuck in the hole was a pole with a white flag whipping in the wind. The house looked as if it had grown straight up out of the ground and refused to be destroyed. But now its roof was puckered. Its sides were green with mold. The drain spouts were rusted and sagging. The shutters looked cockeyed.

Truman whispered, "To build a golf course, don't they have to tear down woodland and any old house that stands in the way? How is it still there?"

"Is this really where Dad grew up?" Camille asked.

"Yes," their mother said, "but he never talked about his childhood much. He never brought me here, not even when we were dating."

Truman always had trouble imagining his parents ever being young, though there were pictures of them, with bigger, puffier hairstyles, on the mantel at home. His mother rubbed her eyes and Truman wondered if she'd teared up. He hated to see her cry. It made his chest tighten, as if he were being hugged too tightly.

"Let's go," Camille said. "It's getting dark."

Truman felt his stomach give one more lurch, as if it had just realized that they'd come to a stop. He grabbed the handle on the door, opened it quickly, and threw up on the pavement.

CHAPTER TWO

The House on the Seventeenth Hole

They made their way across the long sloping stretch of the fairway's trimmed grass in a line—Camille under the weight of her backpack, Truman pulling a suitcase on wheels, and their mother trailing behind. A solitary golfer bobbled by in a golf cart, his golf clubs rattling. He gave the three of them a suspicious glance, but Truman barely noticed. He was staring at the house. It loomed larger and larger the closer they got. In fact, it seemed to rise to meet them.

There, in its dark shadow, was a squat figure with bow legs in thick black stockings sticking out from under a bulky parka. Each breath the person released formed a little cloud in the cold air. It was, of course, Truman and Camille's grandmother. A woman they'd never met and knew only by the disappointing presents she sent for birthdays and holidays— bars of soap, ChapSticks, boxes of crackers. She was standing next to a metal mailbox, dented and dinged over the years by golf balls. Its red metal flag was missing. "Cragmeal" was printed on the side of it in peeling black letters.

She had on a pair of white sneakers that looked like

they'd gotten wet and then had dried in a stiff, odd shape with slightly upturned toes. She carried a gnarled wooden walking stick the way a native in the jungle would hold a spear, as in one of Camille's books on survival. On her head was a wooly blue hat that was lumpy and looked as if it had been made by someone who barely knew how to knit. She tugged at the hat, keeping it snug over her forehead just above her thin white eyebrows. She had a sharp jaw and a noticeable underbite, and when her face sagged and then cinched up tightly, Truman was reminded of a bulldog. (Bulldogs were high on his list of favorite dogs.)

But the most striking thing about their grandmother was her glasses; one of the lenses was completely normal but the other was covered by a shiny black plastic cup. Truman wondered what was wrong with the hidden eye. And he felt his own gaze linger on the plastic cup—longer than he should have let it. His grandmother's other eye caught him staring. It fixed on him with a steely blue concentration. He smiled weakly, fiddling with his inhaler in his coat pocket.

The eye squinted and then blinked and then moved on.

"It's so good to see you," Truman's mother said wearily.

"We haven't seen enough of each other over the years," his grandmother said. "I'm glad I can be of help now . . . now that, well, you know."

Camille sighed loudly. Truman translated the sigh in his head. It went something like: *Oh, so you're going to tiptoe around the subject of our missing father, too, huh? How lovely.*

"This is Truman," his mother said. "And this is Camille. Really growing up, aren't they?"

Truman hated talk about growing. He was pretty sure he'd stopped growing. He was short and slightly pudgy, and he was afraid that the only way he was ever going to grow was horizontally, not vertically.

Their grandmother shook Camille's hand, and then reached for Truman's.

"Careful," Camille said, "he's a barfer."

Their grandmother paused.

"I get carsick," Truman explained.

"Note to self!" their grandmother said. "Barfer." She shook his hand and smiled in a way that suggested she was trying to hide a sudden pang of *What have I signed on for?*

"And here's information on Truman's other medical conditions," his mother said. She handed their grandmother a thick folder.

"Oh my!" their grandmother said.

"Sorry," Truman mumbled under his breath.

"It's all right. I think you might actually do quite well in my house," their grandmother said. And then she looked up at the sky. "Glad you made it before the snow. They've been predicting snow for a week straight, but none comes." Truman looked at the sky through a break in the patchy fog. It looked heavy with gray clouds. "Do you want to come inside and warm up and eat some dinner?"

Truman looked at his mother, as if seeing her for the first time in a long time. She was wearing her navy peacoat with its three oversized buttons. The coat was too big for her. How could his mother look lost even in her own coat? She shook her head. "It's hard enough to say goodbye—even though it won't be too long," she said. "I can't string it out." She pulled a tissue out of her coat pocket and wiped her eyes.

"Don't go all Jell-O on us," Camille said. She was fine with disasters but didn't like plain old emotions. She hadn't cried—not once—since their father left. Truman had cried right away, that first morning when their mother told them at breakfast. He was embarrassed about it, but still, once he started he'd had trouble stopping.

"I'm not! I promise!" their mother said. "I'll call every day. It's only three weeks. It won't be forever. Be good! Okay?" She opened her arms for a hug.

Truman wrapped his arms around her. He'd never gotten the chance to say goodbye to his father. That was one of the hardest parts of it. He breathed in the wooly smell of her coat and tried to memorize it. His father smelled of aftershave, but Truman could barely remember the scent.

After he let go, their mother turned to Camille. "You don't have to hug me if you don't want to," she said. Ever since Camille had given up on her old girly self, their mother gave her a lot of space. She was careful around her.

Camille shrugged as if she didn't care either way. "It's only three weeks. You said so yourself."

"Okay, then," their mother said. "I'll just say, 'See you soon!'" She waited, obviously wanting Camille to change her mind. But Camille only hooked her thumbs around the straps of her backpack and stared at her Converse sneakers. After a moment Truman's mother turned to their grandmother and said, "Thank you again. I can't tell you how much this helps. Once he's home, you know, once he's come back . . ."

"We'll have a party," their grandmother said.

"Exactly," their mother said. "A party." She smiled in a tired way, as if she was barely able to lift the corners of her mouth. Then she gave a small wave, turned, and headed back up the fairway with her pocketbook tucked under her arm.

Truman and Camille stood there, letting their eyes follow her. Truman felt like crying. In fact, he sniffled.

Camille looked at him sharply. "Don't!"

"It's just pollen allergies," Truman said, even though there wasn't really a pollen issue in winter.

Camille rolled her eyes.

"Well," their grandmother said.

They turned around and there she stood before them—this strange-looking woman with her curl-toed sneakers and her ugly woolen hat, sizing them up with her one visible eye. The house looming at her back looked even worse up close—more pocked and dinged by golf balls, more slouched and weathered. "I'm not used to children," she said.

"That's okay," Camille said. "We're not used to old people."

Truman winced. Camille had a way of saying the wrong thing. She was too blunt. But their grandmother gave an appreciative nod, as if she liked this answer. "Let me take you for a tour," she said, digging her walking stick into the ground and heading across the yard.

Camille followed her. But Truman wanted to run back toward the fairway to catch up with his mother, tell her that this was a mistake, that they should stick together as a family now. But he knew that it wouldn't do any good.

He started following Camille and their grandmother. He was still pulling his suitcase, which kept tipping over in the grass. He followed them as quickly as he could, but then let himself glance over his shoulder one last time to see his mother before she left. But she was already gone—a ghostly figure that was lost in the thick fog. *Swallowed*, Truman thought. *Swallowed by the fog.* Maybe he'd been right after all. Maybe Swallow Road wasn't named after the bird.

CHAPTER THREE

The Tour Begins

"I don't like the term *grandmother*. It sounds old, like someone who belongs in a rocker and can only bake pies," their grandmother said. "Plus, I haven't been much of a grandmother to you. I haven't seen you since you were babies, sharing a crib. I looked into your small wobbly eyes. You were so tiny." She paused as if remembering it all in great detail. "But I'm a stranger to you now. Aren't I? A stranger more or less. Why don't you just use my real name? Swelda." She looked at the two of them. "Try it out," she said.

Truman and Camille glanced at each other and then they both said, "Swelda."

She waited expectantly, as if they'd said her name to get her attention. "What is it?" she asked.

"You told us to say your name," Camille said. "So we did."

"Even so, we've established that I'm a stranger to you and you to me, and you don't have a single question?"

The only question Truman could think of was: *What kind of a name is Swelda?*

Camille looked at the embattled house and around the grounds. She said simply, "If you were stranded on a deserted island with only a piece of flint, what would you do?" This was a typical Camille question these days.

"I have been stranded almost all my life," Swelda answered. "This is my deserted island." She banged her walking stick on the ground. "And you know what I've done?"

"No," Camille said.

Swelda lowered her wizened face. "I've survived," she said. "You will too, when the time comes."

Truman didn't know what she'd meant. They'd survive too, when the time came? Survive what? Truman wasn't good at surviving even picnics. (He'd been carted away from the last one due to a pollen/asthma/collision-with-an-errant-Frisbee fiasco.)

The three of them walked across the lawn. And then Swelda stopped and waved her walking stick at the golf course. "In this idiotic game of balls and clubs and loudly colored pants, the golfers must get from the seventeenth tee box to the seventeenth hole. Here, they have to go around this house," she explained loudly. "And they don't aim well! So don't be surprised if you wake up in the morning to the sound of golf balls popping off the roof. Louder than acorns, I tell you! I've boarded up the windows. Tired of replacing the glass! Golfers tee off at five a.m. I hope you two are early risers!"

"I'm an early riser," Camille said. "There's no use just lying in bed dreaming."

"Mmm," Swelda said, as if Camille had given the correct

answer on a test. "Good." And then she peered at Truman intently through her single uncovered lens. "What about you?" she asked.

Truman loved the early-morning fogginess when he couldn't quite tell whether he was dreaming or awake. The mornings were the best time of day to pretend that his father was still living at home, was maybe even in the kitchen frying bacon. "I like to sleep in," he said.

Swelda eyed him suspiciously with her one eye, as if he were some strange new animal that looked familiar but she couldn't quite name. She gave a grunt. "I'll have to keep an extra eye on you." Truman wondered whether she had extra eyes, fake ones maybe, that she kept in a jar somewhere.

Swelda strode to the clipped grassy edge of the course, just a few feet from the front door. She pointed out the sand trap on one side of the house. "Don't play in there. It isn't the beach, you know." Truman hated beaches. His skin was so pale that he always had to be slathered with a thick coat of sunscreen that got in his eyes and made them water uncontrollably. And then he usually burned anyway. (Camille would lightly apply a single coat and then turn golden.)

On the other side, Swelda showed them a pond. "During certain times of year, that little body of water attracts mean, spiteful geese that litter the grass with goose poop. Steer clear of them."

In front of the house was the green of the seventeenth hole itself, with its tall pole and white flag. "Stay off the green," Swelda said. "Golfers do not like children." Then she paused. "And maybe they're right. It's been so long since I've been with children that I barely remember." She looked at them again, with her head cocked to one side. "You interest me, though. I have to admit that. You seem sturdy enough. Are you curious children?"

"About what?" Camille asked.

"About everything! It's a waste to go through the world without a good dose of awe and wonderment."

"I'm curious," Truman said.

"You're cautious," Camille corrected.

"And do you like questions?" Swelda asked Camille.

"I like answers," she said.

"A straight shooter," Swelda said. "I see."

She stopped at the side of the house and pointed her walking stick at a rusty cellar door. "Browsenberry wine," she said.

"Browsenberry wine?" Camille repeated.

"I brew browsenberry wine in the root cellar. That means there are jugs and glass tubing and the delicate working of fermentation. And there is a set of stairs that leads down to the dirt floor, but the third step—the bottom step, that is— well, it's missing. You shouldn't go into the root cellar, but you will. And when you do, remember there is no third step." Swelda smiled. "I don't recall much about children, but I do know that they end up where they're not supposed to be. And sometimes you are *supposed* to be where you're not supposed to be. That is how things happen. That is how the worlds march forward. Actions lead to other actions." She sighed. "You won't be here long," she said, tugging on the ugly blue hat. "Everything is ticking along, one small mechanism clicking with the next. There is no going backward. Only forward." She looked at the two of them. "Do you understand?"

Camille looked at Truman and then back at their grand-mother. "How the *worlds* march forward? *Worlds?* Plural?"

"That's what I said. That's what I meant." She spoke to them as adults, and what was even more unusual, she spoke to them like she was in the middle of a conversation about something big and important. She tapped her walking stick on the ground and set off toward the front of the house. "Come along," she said.

The fog was rolling in quickly now. Truman paused in the front yard. He could no longer see the clubhouse or even much of the flag at the seventeenth hole. They were lost in white. He wondered how long before the fog rolled down the hill and settled on this house too.

Swelda marched up the front steps and opened the door, which creaked loudly. "This house is going through a difficult time right now," she said. "A sudden decay. But I hope that changes soon. Come in! There's more inside!" She disap-peared into the dark house.

More? Truman thought nervously. He could feel a little rasp in his throat. He stuck his hand in his pocket and let his fingers touch the edge of his inhaler. It hit him now for the first time that this was the house his father had grown up in. He'd lived in this house when he was Truman's age. It was strange to think his father had ever been a kid at all—he was tall and hairy and smelled of the aftershave that Truman could barely remember.

Camille walked up to Truman and whispered, "She's weird. I like her."

"Me too," Truman said.

Camille brushed past him up the front steps, but Truman

paused a moment. Something rustled in the bushes. He thought he saw the shiny black tail of a cat. He let his eyes flit over everything around him then—the rolling fog, the sand trap, the pond, the grass of the seventeenth hole, the boarded-up house with its rusty tin roof, and the yard where he stood, the tall grass snug up to the house's brick, and within the grass, some things glowing in the last bit of dusky light, glowing like eggs—or eyes. But they were only lost golf balls.

CHAPTER FOUR

Imports from a Distant Land

The living room was so dim that Truman felt as if he'd walked into a tunnel. His eyes had trouble adjusting. He pushed his glasses up the bridge of his nose, but that didn't help much.

At first it seemed that glowing orbs were suspended in midair in the corners of the room, but then he saw that they were paper lanterns, gold and blue. They hung above over-stuffed sofas covered in frayed brocade, with ornate wooden arms and feet carved to look like swirling horns. The old pine floor was covered in a wooly white rug.

"These are heirlooms! Antiques!" Swelda's voice rang out. "Imports from distant lands! Keep your mitts to yourselves!"

Truman was sure he was *in* a distant land, someplace foreign. He felt the way immigrants he'd learned about in school must have felt when they first stepped off the boat. The house even smelled foreign—like some strange stew was boiling over somewhere. He couldn't eat strange stews! Too many possibilities for an allergic reaction. He'd have to ask for something bland, like toast.

"Coats go here on the hall tree," Swelda said. Truman

expected an old-fashioned hall tree, they'd had one in their old house—a wooden one with brass hooks. But this hall tree looked like an actual tree, and it seemed to be growing straight up out of the floorboards. On it were a few scattered Christmas ball ornaments, some hats, and an umbrella.

"Is this a real tree?" Truman asked.

"I don't like fake ones," Swelda said.

Camille walked up to it. "It can't be real," she said. "There's this thing called photosynthesis that doesn't work so well in a boarded-up house."

"It's as real as I am," Swelda said.

Camille shrugged off her coat and hung it on one of the tree limbs very carefully. "If it's real," she asked, "where are its leaves?"

"It's winter now," Swelda said. "You can't blame it for not having leaves!"

"It looks a little thirsty," Truman said.

Swelda walked up to it and rubbed one of the limbs. "You're right," she said.

"I think trees do better outside," Camille said.

Swelda didn't seem to hear her. She was examining the tree's trunk very closely, shaking her head.

Truman was standing by a set of bookshelves that held enormous books. He read a few spines: *The Dark and Ignorant Ages; Pre-Exodus: The Complete Understanding: Field Guide to Fire-Breathers; Dendrology: A Gramarye's Dictionary of Terms and Best Practices.*

"Camille," he whispered, "look at these."

"Old tomes!" Swelda said. "It's important to have a reference section at your fingertips."

Camille walked to the bookshelf and let her fingers drift over the bindings. "Reference section?" Camille said, and then she stopped and laid her finger on one enormous book. "*The Breath World*," she read aloud. "*A Complete History*"?

"Would you prefer an incomplete history?" Swelda said. "That wouldn't do you much good, would it."

Truman walked to the middle of the room, and as he turned a slow circle, he stared at the shelves crammed with tins and jars and candles, and at the framed parchment scrolls and old pictures that hung everywhere. One, for example, was a photograph of an exhausted, worn-down family by a stew pot in a ratty hut whose walls were covered with large winged insects; it was labeled "Early Gramarye Settlers in the Ostley Wood: The Plague of Tree Vermin." Another photograph had the caption "Founding Members of the Society of Jarkmen." On a high shelf sat a model of a ship that was being pulled down by a school of suckerfish. An etching—crude but beautiful and rich—was propped under a glass frame; it showed a tree with its web of roots stretching to bind together two worlds. He noticed a large crest on a shield; winding through its center was a snake with flared feathers on its head. Truman was pretty sure that this animal didn't actually exist.

There was also a painting of three snow globes that was hung over the mantel above a dark and musty fireplace. All the globes were full of swirling snow, as if they were being shaken at that very moment even though they were sitting on a table in the painting.

"Why is there nothing to see in these snow globes?" Truman asked.

"There's snow in the snow globes," Swelda said.

"But why just snow?"

"They are called *snow* globes, Truman. What do you expect?"

He expected little winter scenes, as in every other snow globe he'd ever seen, but he knew there was no use arguing with Swelda. He moved along to a photograph in a small gilded frame. "Who's in this picture?" Truman asked, pointing to a framed photograph of two girls—identical twins—a little younger than himself and Camille. The twins were dressed in pale skirts with dark sashes, and they were standing in a field, holding a hoop. They each had a patch over one eye. A third girl, smaller than the other two, had poked her head in the middle of the hoop, trying to hog the spotlight. Twins—like him and Camille. Truman was always kind of fascinated by identical twins, because he and Camille weren't—even though, oddly enough, when they said they were twins, people often asked, "Are you identical?" Sometimes Truman would answer yes, just to watch it settle in.

"That's me on the left," Swelda said. But then she squinted, walked over to the photograph, picked it up, and said, "No, no. That's me on the right or . . . then again . . . Well, I'm *one* of them!" She propped the photograph back up on the shelf. "I was young once too, you know."

Swelda had hung her parka on the hall tree as well. But she hadn't taken off the blue hat. She'd only pushed it to the back of her head, revealing puffs of white hair. "The other girl is my twin, of course. That's our homeland. She stayed behind and I came here."

Camille walked over and stared at the photograph too.

"And who's the one in the middle, looking through the hoop?" Camille asked. The little girl was holding a jar of insects of some sort, with holes popped into the lid.

"That's Milta. She is our sadness. We carry her in our sad sack," Swelda said.

"Sad sack?" Camille asked.

"All of us must carry our own sad sack around with us. That's why we all look so tired sometimes."

Truman thought of his mother. She was tired from carrying her sadness, that was a fact. He looked at the girl in the photograph and noticed a scar on her cheek—a curlicue scar, a dainty spiral. "What happened to her face?"

"A run-in with a bad gramarye when she was a child," Swelda said. "A nasty one. I still feel guilty about that. Ickbee and I were supposed to be watching her."

"What's a gramarye?" Truman asked.

Swelda stared at them, shocked, with her one eye wide and round. "Hasn't your father ever even whispered a thing about our family?"

Truman and Camille weren't sure what to say. They shrugged. "He *kind of* has," Truman said. He turned to Camille. "Remember when we had to do that report in second grade about our heritage?"

"He told us we were immigrants," Camille said.

Swelda started muttering to herself. "It's my fault. I didn't encourage it enough! I let him let go of it all for love. I . . . I'm sorry."

"That's okay," Truman said, not exactly sure what he was forgiving.

"My sister Milta could be anywhere . . . it's hard when

people leave unexpectedly," Swelda said. "I understand how that feels."

Camille shifted nervously and dug her hands into her pockets. Truman didn't say anything. He missed his father, and now he felt as if he'd been abandoned again, by his mother this time. It wasn't true. He knew she'd come back, but still . . .

"Where is your homeland?" Camille asked, changing the subject.

"It's *not* Brooklyn and it's *not* Boca Raton," Swelda answered. "It's *not* a lot of places. But it's hard to say exactly what it *is*. Your father was right, though. We are immigrants."

"Do you miss it?" Truman asked, missing his own house with the card table in the kitchen and the heating vents that let him eavesdrop and his own bedroom with his collection of bobbleheads.

"No, I don't miss it," she said. "We all make decisions in this life. Some are for good!"

Truman thought about his father. Was his decision to leave for good? Would he ever come back?

"So you're glad you left?" Camille asked.

Swelda, her blue eye almost glowing in the pale light from one of the lanterns, looked at Camille. "I love my homeland with all of my heart, and I hate it just the same."

"But how can you love something with all of your heart and hate it too?" Truman asked.

"The world is full of contradictions. Do you think the world is simple? Have you already figured it all out?" She put her hands on her hips and stared at him.

"No," Truman said. He remembered his father—how he had lingered in the doorway of Truman and Camille's bedroom the night before he left. (The kids shared a room divided by a sheet strung between the beds.) He sang them a lullaby—the one Camille complained about because she said they were too old for it—the same one every night. The chorus went like this:

> *Sleep, slumber, sweet slumber ba-ru.*
> *Sleepy-seed, sleepy-seed, dew.*
> *Snug cover and pillow, hear the hush of the willow*
> *And I will stand dream watch over you.*

Their father usually said "Good night" and shut the door—though not all the way. But that last night, he stayed there in the doorway until Truman and Camille fell asleep. It was the last time either of them would see him before he disappeared, but they didn't know that then.

Now when Truman thought of the lullaby, it only made him angry. His father wasn't keeping dream watch over him. Truman loved his father with all of his heart. But how could he have left them without any word? Sometimes Truman's chest felt heavy, as if it had taken on some angry leaden weight, and even though he knew it was wrong, he felt that he hated his father too.

Swelda raised her crooked finger in the air. "Be wary of anyone who tells you that the world is simple," she said. "Be wary of anyone who hands you simple answers to complex problems."

Camille walked to the bookshelves again.

"I don't think you'll understand any of those books," Swelda said.

"What's mundivagation?" Camille asked.

"See what I mean?" Swelda said.

Camille continued along the rows, moving from one book to the next. But Truman couldn't focus. His eyes seemed to shoot off in all directions and his thoughts were jumping all around like a bunch of frogs. He walked over to a mossy exotic fern with fuzzy pink flowers dangling from its webby fronds. Looking at it closely, he thought he saw an eye—a small beady eye—staring out at him. He pushed a frond out of the way to reveal the eye, which was embedded in the hunched feathery head of a vulture with a red beak. He gasped and clattered backward, bumping into Camille at the bookcase.

"Hey, watch it!" she said.

"A vulture!" he said, breathlessly.

"It's a fake," Swelda said. "A shrunken, stuffed-animal version. In real life, these vultures are massive. You can be afraid of it all you want, but fear is a waste of time."

"It's good to be afraid sometimes," Truman said defensively. "If we weren't afraid, we'd be idiots!"

"Truman doesn't like to step outside his comfort zone," Camille told Swelda. "He's the King of Fear. He couldn't run with scissors."

"I could too run with scissors," he said. "If something awful was chasing me."

"Awful?" Camille said. "Like a bunny?"

This was a cheap shot. A few years earlier, Truman had refused to sit on the Easter Bunny's lap at the mall to have his picture taken.

"I'm tougher than you think!" Truman said hotly, annoyed that his sister even brought that up.

"You're even tougher than *you* think, Truman," Swelda said.

The vulture had glistening glass eyes that seemed to follow him as he backed away from it to the far side of the room. But once there he spotted another stuffed bird, sitting in a cage this time. This one was a white parrot with a fan of feathers on its head. It wasn't as terrifying as the vulture. In fact, he liked this one. To prove that he was tougher than Camille thought, he put his finger in between the bars of the cage to touch its white feathers. Just then, the parrot squawked, and Truman screamed.

"That one's alive, though," Swelda said. "Yes, he's quite alive."

Camille laughed.

Truman glared at her.

The parrot used his beak to lift the door to his cage, then made his way, claw over claw, to the outside of the cage.

"Here, Grossbeak!" Swelda called. The bird gave a few strong flaps of his wings and lifted himself into the air, circling the ceiling and then, finally, perching on Swelda's shoulder. "Out of this room, you two. Come along now. Follow me!"

CHAPTER FIVE

The Tasting Tale

"Gladwell biscuits, apple-dipped jelly yolks, whipped maca-
roons in a charred-prill sauce," their grandmother said, holding
a silver platter heaped with steaming food. "Broiled tubers,
aspergillus gluten spread on sea-sprayed chowder chips! Pear
noodles, minced toffee-dipped choy! Lemon-dotted fiddle-
faddle! More and more! To drink? Seventeen types of tea."

Truman and Camille gazed at the platter. It was stacked
so high with food that they could see only the blue tuft of
their grandmother's hat sticking out on the other side. The
rest of the kitchen was simple, spare, cramped—with an ancient stove and a leaky faucet that was tapping a rust spot in
the sink. There was a small round table with two place set-
tings and two chairs. Grossbeak was perched on top of the refrigerator, where he occasionally squawked.

Truman didn't recognize a single type of food on the platter. Not one.

"Truman here," Camille said, "is allergic to everything.
His face blows up like a blimp. You should refer to his folder
of medical records."

"My stomach's still a little loopy from the car trip," he said.

"There's nothing here that Truman will be allergic to. I import all of my ingredients," Swelda said. "I guarantee he'll be fine."

Swelda couldn't have cross-checked the meal with his records. She just got his records!

"Really?" Truman said. "One hundred percent money-back guarantee?"

She nodded.

"Still, this can't all be for us," Camille said.

"Of course it is," Swelda said.

"We can't eat all of this," Truman said.

"We're not sumo wrestlers," Camille added.

"It's not for eating. It's for tasting." Swelda, staggering under the platter's weight, shuffled to the kitchen table, which held a curved row of teacups, all partially filled and sitting in saucers. She lowered the platter.

"This is a vegetarian meal," she said. "Once you've spoken with an animal, you can't eat it."

"Have you spoken with animals?" Truman asked.

"I think she's speaking figuratively," Camille said.

Swelda sighed. "I forget sometimes that you two only know what little you know. Sit down!"

Truman and Camille slid into the two chairs.

"I'm not really all that hungry," Truman said.

"He's hyperallergic and hyperpicky," Camille translated.

"That's why I made so many kinds of food," Swelda said. "So you can pick your way through them." She whipped two cloth napkins off the table and plopped them onto the kids' laps. Handing them each a pair of tongs and a plate, she said, "While you taste, I will tell you a tale."

"A story, you mean?" Truman asked.

"It's called a tasting tale," Swelda explained. "The kind that's told to you while you eat."

"Is this an old family tradition?" Truman asked, thinking about his father's childhood.

"It is. Our people, especially us Cragmeals, have always told tasting tales so that people could link each part of the story with a certain food—hold the story on their tongue, and then swallow it piece by piece."

"What's the story about?" Camille asked.

"When the first sliver of food sits in your mouth, I'll begin."

Camille dug her tongs in first—into mounds of strangely colored bobbles and bits from the various bowls and plates. Then she used the serving spoons to scoop the soupier items.

Truman wasn't sure what to pick first. He let his tongs hover. Everything looked too foreign—too gooey or too dry or too blackened or too wet. He winced and then picked up a shiny yellow ball and put it on his plate.

"A little bit of everything," Swelda goaded.

"But—"

"No buts. Just a little taste of everything."

He did as he was told and picked up one of each thing— a biscuit, a spoonful of whipped beets, a chowder chip—all of it. Camille had already started eating.

"Mmm," she said. "This is amazing!"

Once Truman's plate was full, he set it down in front of himself. He paused, plucked a teacup from the row, and set it in front of himself too, just in case he had to wash something down quickly. He then closed his eyes and let his fingers walk across the plate. They landed on something sticky and doughy and light. Without looking at it, he held it to his nose and sniffed.

Truman held his breath and popped the thing into his mouth. It tasted like nothing he'd ever tried before. It was tangy and gummy and bittersweet, but also sharp. It tingled his nose the way soda sometimes did, but there weren't any bubbles. He took another bite, and this time it was more sugary and brittle and warm. He didn't feel itchy or tight in his throat. His nose didn't start running. He didn't have a headache. He felt good—maybe a little warm in his chest, but as if he'd come in from the cold and was starting to thaw out.

He looked over at Camille and she looked dazed, as if she were daydreaming while she chewed.

Swelda began to tell her tale:

"Once upon a time, when the world was so new that the sky still showed its stitching—"

"Oh, so this isn't a true story," Camille whispered, dreamily.

"Another thing about the tasting tale, you can't interrupt the teller, because it's impolite to speak with your mouth full."

"Sorry," Camille mumbled.

"Once upon a time, there was only one world for all of us. All those magical creatures—the ones you see now only in dreams and stories—used to walk among us. But just as light was separated from darkness, for reasons we don't understand and never will, the magical creatures were separated from the rest and two worlds were created."

The tastes that filled Truman's mouth were hard to

describe. They were sour and then tart. They lingered in his mouth and then suddenly swelled into a bitter tang. A salty taste like seawater would spike into a rich coffee taste and then become comforting, as simple as milk.

"The moon passed over the sun and the day went dark, and when the light started to slip back onto the face of the earth, the magical creatures were gone. They stirred only in people's dreams, imaginations, and distant collective memories."

The textures of the foods were just as changeable. Some of the foods were gummy. Others were crisp. Others melted in Truman's mouth like dollops of honey the moment they hit his tongue.

"The two worlds are still unified in a mysterious way," Swelda continued, her voice dropping to a whisper. "Sometimes it's hard to determine whether our dreams direct our lives or our lives direct our dreams. Isn't it?"

Their cheeks stuffed with food, Truman and Camille both nodded. Yes, yes, it was.

"This is the Fixed World. This world we live in now. And the other world was named the Breath World. Those in the Breath World felt cast out, of course, and so a stone to control the balance and flow between the two worlds was placed in their world. A stone called the Ever Breath—an amber orb with a breath embedded in its very center."

Truman looked up at her, confused. *Breath?* he wanted to say. *In a stone?*

Swelda paused and then sat back. "You want to know whose breath it is in the stone. Don't you?"

He nodded.

"We don't know, Truman. There are lots of names for

this being. I tend to call this being A Being Than Which Nothing Greater Can Be Conceived. The name arose centuries ago, but this being can go by any name. This particular name is a long one, but it works for me. Is that okay with you, Truman?"

He thought about this: *A Being Than Which Nothing Greater Can Be Conceived.* He nodded.

She put her bony elbows on the table and leaned in. "But if the Ever Breath is taken from its rightful spot, the passage between the two worlds begins to wither, and if it's not returned, the two worlds will be closed off from each other forever. Which means that there can be no magical thinking in the Fixed World, no imagination, no more dreaming."

How could this be? How could anyone be cut off from dreams, from imagination? The thought buzzed around in his head. He felt panic rise up in his chest. He glanced at Camille, and her face looked pale. Her eyes were wide. It was only a story, wasn't it? Why, then, did it seem so true?

Truman looked down at his plate. The food had thinned out. Camille's plate was nearly empty too. He nibbled at a fruit-encrusted heel of bread. Camille popped a few remaining purple seeds.

"That would mean death," Swelda said. "This world would die."

Truman squinted at Swelda. Was he hearing her right? Her voice sounded echoey and dim.

"This world cannot survive without magical thinking, imagination, and dreams," she said.

And the Breath World? Truman wondered.

She answered his question as if he'd said it aloud. "The Breath World would lose its tether to the Fixed World, its anchor, and it would have no place to send its overflow of magic. The imagination would take over in its darkest forms. The evil magical beasts would rise up and take over. It would destroy itself."

Truman tried to imagine that as well, but he couldn't. It was too terrifying to think of worlds ending, and his mind felt cloudy. He licked one of his fingers and dabbed at the crumbs.

The room fell silent.

"Go on," Camille whispered. "Tell us more."

"I would tell you more, but your plates are empty and your stomachs full and your mouth has flown open. That's how I know that the tasting tale is finished." Swelda lifted the platter. It was still laden with food—beautiful savory juicy sweet food! They'd barely made a dent, but she was right. Truman was full. He couldn't eat another bite. He was thirsty, though. He emptied teacup after teacup—orangey bitters, strong berry flavors, various mint mixes—and Camille did too. It was as if they were overcome with thirst.

When they put down the last cups, the story was swirling inside of them. There were two worlds. The Fixed World— this house with its boarded-up windows and everywhere they knew—and the Breath World.

Swelda started to pack the food up into little containers as if it had been an ordinary meal in an ordinary house. "Your bedroom is upstairs at the end of the hall," she said. "It's your father's old bedroom, where he slept as a boy." Swelda seemed a little embarrassed for a moment. Then she quickly added, "And there's a gift sitting on each of the pillows."

Soap? Truman thought, remembering the gifts she'd sent to them for years. *Crackers, ChapStick?* Was this even the same woman whom he'd known only by her horrible gifts? Everything seemed different now.

Swelda came to them and gently cupped each of their faces with her small hands for a moment. She smiled, her lower jaw more prominent than before. Her face was so close that they could see the fine wrinkles around her eyes, the delicate folds of skin on her neck. "You are Cragmeals," she said. "From the long line."

"The long line?" Truman said.

"I knew you'd show up here, in this house, one day." Swelda's one eye twinkled, wet with tears. And then she let go of their faces. She tapped her plastic cup, which blocked one of her eyes, with one nail—*tick, tick, tick.* "I've seen it all coming!"

"Seen what coming?" Camille asked.

Swelda didn't answer. She heaved a sigh as she shuffled, as if tired now, to the sink and leaned against it, her back to them. Then she looked at them briefly over her shoulder.

"Keep your eyes on those gifts," she said. "Keep your eyes on them!"

Truman turned to Camille. Were they supposed to go to their bedrooms now? They looked at Swelda's narrow back. The parrot, Grossbeak, flew around the kitchen and then perched on her shoulder. They could see his eye, and the flared plumage on his head, which was cocked to one side.

"Bye-bye," the parrot squawked. "Bye-bye, knucklehead!"

"Who, me?" Truman whispered.

"Well, I'm not a knucklehead, so he's not talking to me!" Camille said.

"Bye-bye," Truman said to the parrot softly. He wanted to add *knucklehead,* but he didn't.

CHAPTER SIX

The Gifts

The wallpaper running up the walls of the staircase had water stains that took on strange shapes in the low light. As Truman followed Camille, he thought he saw a face in the water stains and then a dog. Not just any dog. This water stain looked like a Chinese fighting dog with lots of wrinkles and a smushed face. He stopped and touched the water stain with one hand. This close, he could see that it also seemed to have wings and horns and fangs, as if it were a dog-sized dragon. "The Breath World." He whispered the words and wondered if this was the kind of magical creature that would live there.

"Are you feeling the wallpaper?" Camille said from the doorway at the end of the hall.

"Of course not," Truman said.

She disappeared into the bedroom and Truman followed her. The room was spare, with two twin beds covered with nubby white blankets. Two brass sconces attached to the walls were glowing dimly. In one corner was a wingback arm-chair and in the other corner were a small desk and a chair.

"This is it, I guess," Camille said. She looked a little

disappointed. Truman was too. He'd been hoping that the room would have more of their father's childhood left in it.

The bright spot, though, was that there were two gifts, just as Swelda had said. On each of the pillows was a plain white box.

"Our gifts," Truman said. He walked to the bed and picked up one of the boxes. This one had his name scrawled on top in thick black ink. "What do you think they are?"

"Well, I would have said jars of tacks or sticks of glue, but now I don't know," Camille said. "The story she told us . . ."

"It seemed like it was true," Truman said.

"But it couldn't have been," Camille said, shaking her head. "She may not like the term *grandmother*, but she is one. And grandmothers *invented* fairy tales, didn't they? You know, to stop kids from taking shortcuts through the woods and eating apples offered by strangers." She sat down in the wingback. "But when I asked about her homeland, she didn't answer me. Did you notice that?"

"I want to know where she imported all that food from. I ate everything and I feel fine."

"Yeah," Camille said. "I was sure you'd turn into a Macy's Parade balloon."

Truman turned the box in his hands. He wanted it to be something special. Something *truly* special. He was tired of disappointment. Every morning when he woke up, he hoped that that day would be the one when his father came home. But each day passed with no Dad.

"I'm opening my gift," he said.

"No, wait. We'll open them together," Camille said.

Because they were twins, they were used to opening presents at the same time.

Camille got up, went to the other bed, and picked up her box. Then she and Truman sat across from each other and said, in unison, "One, two, three!"

They popped open the lids.

Inside each of the boxes, a little note sat on top of tissue paper.

Truman unfolded his and read aloud:

"'There are only three true seeing globes in the worlds. This one once belonged to my sister Ickbee. And now it is yours. Let it guide you. Love, Swelda.'"

He looked at Camille. "A *seeing* globe?"

Camille pulled out her note and read it:

"'This once was mine. It is one of three in the worlds enchanted for seeing. It now belongs to you—with all the power and all the responsibility that come with it. Love, Swelda.'"

Camille rubbed her forehead. "Enchanted!" she said. "Does she think we're second-graders?"

"I don't know, but I hope this isn't more crackers or Chap-Stick." Truman reached past the crinkly white tissue paper and felt something cool and smooth and round and heavy.

He lifted it from the box.

It was a glass snow globe, as big as a baby's head.

Camille pulled out a snow globe of her own.

They both shook their globes, and the snow swirled up.

"Look at this," Camille said, holding hers to the light. "A little mud hut that seems to be covered with roots and vines." The little house was situated in a dense forest, with trees crowding around it. "And look," she said, "there's an old woman peeking out of one of the windows." They could see only half of the woman's face; the other half was hidden behind a yellow curtain. Camille squinted. "It looks like she has two cats sitting on her shoulders." She paused. "No," she said, "three cats. Maybe four."

Truman held up his globe. The snow had settled. He and Camille peered at the miniature landscape inside. There was a large tent, its flaps billowing in the watery wind.

There was a young man in a blue hat who seemed to have stumbled backward and fallen on the ground beside a round cage that held a straggly dog. A woman with dark skin—dry and cracked, as if mud-caked—stood over him. She was dressed in a hooded cloak. On the ground between, there lay a knife, its hilt in the shape of a snake's head with the flared feathers of a parrot.

"It's like Grossbeak's head, but on a snake," Truman said.

"And look at his hat," Camille said.

It was wooly, much like their grandmother's hat. "That's strange," Truman said.

They both inched even closer to the globe. The man on the ground was wearing a white shirt, but it was turning red—a bright spot of blood was spreading across his white shirt!

Keep your eyes on those gifts, Truman heard his grandmother's voice repeat in his head. *Keep your eyes on them!*

CHAPTER SEVEN

Into the Cold, Dark Night

Truman couldn't sleep that night. The room shifted with strange shadows, and the narrow bed squeaked every time he moved. He lay on his side and stared at his snow globe sitting on the bedside table. Even now, just sitting there, it shimmered. Had the woman in the hooded cloak stabbed the man on the ground? What kind of grandmother gives a snow globe like that as a gift? *My grandmother*, Truman thought.

Camille was having no trouble at all sleeping. She was even snoring a little, cradling her snow globe like a football.

Truman always had trouble falling asleep. When he closed his eyes, his mind would be flooded with strange creatures—roaring, clawing, creeping, pouncing. His father called his imagination his blessing and his curse. But it seemed like just a curse to Truman.

In addition to the strange room with its strange noises and shadows and the eerie image in the snow globe, Truman was being kept up by his stomach. It was gurgling. He wasn't sure how it was possible, but he was hungry. And he'd just eaten more than he ever had in his entire life!

As he tossed and turned, he only felt hungrier and hungrier. Eventually, at some point after midnight, it dawned on him that he hadn't really *eaten* dinner. He'd *tasted* it! It had been a *tasting* tale! There were tons of food left over too, in all those containers. He put on his glasses, kicked off his blanket, and decided to go downstairs for a late-night snack.

He took the snow globe with him. He could stare at it while he ate—maybe he'd see something that made sense. He wanted desperately to connect the snow globe to the story Swelda had told.

He tiptoed out into the hallway and passed Swelda's shut door. He could hear her snoring too, loudly. He was glad she was asleep. He was embarrassed by his pajamas— blue flannel with red buttons. Who had buttons on their pajamas anymore?

He ran his hand along the water-stained wallpaper—the dragonlike Chinese fighting dog—as he went down the stairs. The living room was dark, but he could see the dim shapes of the furniture, as well as the hall tree standing quietly by the door. It looked a bit drier than it had the day before.

When he stepped into the kitchen, he felt the wall for a light switch. He patted the spot where the light switch was at home, but there was nothing. He patted a bit more. Still nothing. And then, as if by magic, the overhead lights shone bright.

And there, claws gripped to the back of a chair, was Grossbeak. His perch was mounted on the wall right next to a light switch. The wall had a long, wide crack running all the way to the ceiling. Truman didn't remember seeing it when he'd been in the kitchen the day before. Was it possible he hadn't noticed a crack that big? Did it just appear, like a crack shooting through the ice on a frozen lake?

Truman looked at the crack and then the light switch and then the parrot. "Did you turn the lights on?" Truman asked, imagining him pecking it with his fat, curved beak.

Grossbeak bobbed his head.

"Did you just nod at me?" Truman asked.

Grossbeak bobbed his head again.

"You're a smart bird, aren't you?"

"Parrot, knucklehead!" Grossbeak squawked, correcting him.

"You know it's not nice to call people knucklehead, right?"

Grossbeak bobbed his head. He knew all right. And then he added, "Knucklehead!"

Truman gave him a dirty look and walked to the fridge. He opened the door. The containers were stacked everywhere. Truman was delighted. He recalled, immediately, the tastes of the different foods, and with each remembered taste, a bit of the story swirled within him too. He remembered the strange dizziness of the tale, the way it felt inside him. He wanted that feeling back again.

And he realized that he wasn't hungry for the food— or not just for the food. He was really hungry for more of the story.

Feeling greedy, he picked up a mini-tower of containers, turned around with his arms full, and shut the refrigerator door with an elbow. He set the containers on the table.

Grossbeak glared at him, flaring his head feathers.

45

"What?" Truman asked, innocently. "I'm just getting a snack, that's all."

The parrot shook his head.

"Do you have a problem with that?" Truman asked, spreading the containers around on the table, trying to decide which one to open first.

Grossbeak nodded. His scaly feet paced back and forth on the back of the chair.

"Too bad," Truman said.

But when Truman pulled up the corner of a lid, the bird squawked viciously and beat his wings, lifting his body off the chair. He flapped in a circle over Truman's head.

"Hey!" Truman shouted, covering his head with his arms. "Stop it!"

But the parrot only became more vicious, snapping his beak and squawking. He flew up toward the ceiling again, but this time he dive-bombed.

Truman grabbed his snow globe and took off running. He sprinted one lap around the tiny kitchen, the parrot flapping wildly behind him, and then darted into the dark living room.

Truman stumbled. Everything went quiet for a moment. He thought he might be able to hide here. The bird seemed to have disappeared into the shadows.

But suddenly, in a gusty flap of wings, he was there again, right in front of Truman's face, snapping his beak as if he were testing the amount of force it would take to peck a boy to death. His wings stirred a breeze so strong that it rippled Truman's hair and shirt.

Truman darted behind furniture and curtains. "Back off!"

he shouted. He knew his sister would sleep right through all of his yelling. Was Swelda the same? Could anyone hear him?

He dodged and parried, and eventually he wound up near the front door. The bird blocked him in, massive wings beating, plumage flared. Truman saw no way to escape him— except through the front door, out into the night.

Truman struggled with the lock and the doorknob, but at last the door swung open. Truman slammed it shut behind him.

It was dark outside, except for a distant floodlight on the golf course. It had started to snow. The scene was dusted in white, much like the one in the snow globe that Truman still had tucked under one arm.

Barefoot and wearing only his pajamas, Truman stood on the front stoop, wondering how he'd get back inside, past Grossbeak, to his bed. And then he heard a pecking noise on the other side of the door, and a click.

"Grossbeak?" he said.

Truman turned the knob.

The door was locked.

CHAPTER EIGHT

Through the Passageway

Truman hugged the snow globe to his chest and tried to wrap his arms around himself to keep warm. He started hopping from foot to foot to keep the snow from stinging his bare feet. The snow was coming down fast. The flakes were heavy and fat, and the fog was so thick that Truman could see only a few feet in front of his nose. Everything was white. His glasses fogged up too, so it was like trying to see a cloud through a cloud. He pulled them off and wiped them on his pajama top, but as soon as he put them back on they fogged up again.

He wondered if he should pound on the door and call for help. But would Swelda and Camille even wake up? Or would this just rile Grossbeak?

Truman remembered the lost golf balls he'd seen earlier. He could dig for some golf balls in the grass and throw them at the boarded-up windows. It was all he could think of, and he had to try *something*. He couldn't stay out here all night!

As he walked down the brick steps, he felt the edges crumble just a bit beneath his feet. Was the house about to collapse?

He tiptoed through the snow to the deep grass near the bushes where he'd seen golf balls earlier. The grass was stiff with cold.

Then he heard a small cry. It rose up in the night air. Two sad notes: *mewl-mewl*. Like a cat, but not quite. The voice was sadder, more human.

"Mewl-mewl," it cried again.

Truman remembered the shiny black tail of the cat he thought he'd seen in the bushes when they first arrived. Was the cat still lost out here in the cold?

"Here, kitty," he called. "Here, kitty, kitty."

The cat cried again, in that nearly human voice. Truman could see only white and the clouded outlines of the nearby bushes, the edge of the house. The cry sounded even farther away, like it was coming from the side yard. He followed the voice. "It's going to be okay," he called.

Truman kept one hand on the side of the house so as not to lose his bearings. The fog was rolling in even more heavily. Now he could see only a white mistiness.

"Mewl-mewl," the cat cried. This time it sounded like it had turned another corner and was coming in from the backyard.

"I'm coming," Truman called. "Stay still." He'd decided that, even though he was allergic to pet dander, he'd pick the cat up and bring it inside—however he could get inside. Maybe it was a kitten that had gotten separated from its mother and was now lost in the freezing cold. He would heat up some milk and put it in a saucer.

Truman was in the backyard now, blinded by whiteness.

He could see the small glowing cracks between the boards nailed over the windows in the kitchen. But that was all.

"Here, kitty, kitty, kitty," he called again.

But there was no answer.

He turned in a circle, calling, "Here, kitty, kitty, kitty." Again, nothing.

His feet were so cold they felt like they were burning. His face stung. Would the water in his snow globe freeze out here and break the glass? He held on to the snow globe more tightly. He wasn't sure what to do. Just then, Grossbeak must have pecked at the light switch in the kitchen, because the lit cracks between the boards went dark.

And all at once Truman felt like crying. He realized, for the first time, how alone he was—not just because his father had disappeared and not just because his mother had left him here. Not just because his sister and grandmother couldn't hear him. No. He felt really and truly alone in the world. Lost and alone.

But then he heard the warbled cry of the cat, one more time. "Mewl-mewl." It sounded muffled, like it was coming from somewhere in the house. That was when Truman remembered the root cellar—the place where Swelda made her browsenberry wine.

One hand holding the snow globe, he held the other out in front of his face and walked, blindly, toward the sound of the cat's cry. He padded the snow with one outstretched foot before taking each step. And finally his toe felt the stiff lip of the root cellar door, which thankfully was propped open. He quickly walked down the steps: the first step, the second step—and then there was nothing there, only air where a step should be. He landed so hard on the dirt floor that the wind was knocked out of him. He remembered the missing third step that Swelda had warned him and Camille about. What if he had an asthma attack in here? His inhaler was inside his jeans pocket in the bedroom.

As he stood up, still trying to catch his breath, something brushed his face. He batted it away, but it swung back. He grabbed it and realized that it was a string. To a light? He pulled it.

A bare lightbulb dangling from the ceiling brightened the room.

Now he could see why it was called a root cellar. The dirt walls were entwined with roots, like thick ropes, knots, and bulbous joints. They curled all around the cellar, leading out from one specific spot—the base of a tree. The hall tree! Here was its base, living and breathing, inside his grandmother's dark root cellar. A miracle of a tree.

There were also rows of bottles on shelves lining the walls and wide wooden barrels and kettles, crocks, strainers, and funnels—all for brewing browsenberry wine, he figured.

Truman walked over to a table in the middle of the room. It was covered with yeast sacks, gears, a bucket of corks, fine woven cloth, and tools he couldn't name. In the corner, in large baskets, were the berries themselves—so pale they looked like small, bright full moons. Truman dipped his hand into a basket of the cool fruits. He could feel the soft prickle of their fine downy fur, soft as peach fuzz. He realized that he was breathing in calm, regular breaths.

And then the cry. "Mewl-mewl."

He'd almost forgotten the cat! He looked around the edges of the root cellar and caught a glimpse of it darting along the far wall before it slipped into a hole dug in the dirt amid a network of vines.

Truman walked to the hole, got down on his knees, and tried to peer into the darkness. "Come on out!" he called. "I'll keep you safe."

He couldn't see anything and so he reached into the hole, clutching the snow globe with his other arm. His hand slid down a steep and crumbling tunnel lined with bumpy roots.

"Where are you?" he whispered. "What kind of tunnel is this?" He let his arm follow his hand and then let his head— chin tucked—and his chest follow.

He heard the cat mewl, but now it sounded like she was saying "Follow, follow."

Truman crawled down this strange, dark root-lined tunnel. The tunnel seemed to widen ever so slightly, but still he felt like he was being swallowed by the dirt. He thought back to the day before, when they were looking for his grandmother's house. Swallow Road. He thought of Swelda's tasting tale—the one he'd swallowed piece by piece. His heart raced in his chest. Would he be able to get back out of here?

It was too late to worry about that. The tunnel narrowed now, and he had to crawl on his elbows.

"Follow, follow," he heard again.

The tunnel was tight, and the roots dug into his bony knees, but up ahead he saw something glowing.

He crawled more quickly.

It was a wine bottle glowing like a lamp. The label read "Swelda's Browsenberry Wine." Up ahead he saw another glowing bottle and then another and another. He kept following them on his belly through the dirt, until he heard mewling again. But it wasn't just one voice. It was many voices, all mewling at the same time.

Then, without warning, the tunnel widened into a round room. The ceiling was suddenly tall enough for him to stand up. A tall root, straight as a post, shot up from the earth. It was encircled by glowing jars. The root was thin and delicate, with five thin offshoots that formed a hand: four long branchlike fingers and one thick thumb. It was poised as if it should be holding an apple up in the air. But it was empty. And the pinky on the hand looked brittle and was curling slightly inward, as if injured.

Truman stepped around the jars. Although the room was dug out of the earth and wrapped in roots, it seemed like a sacred place. Where *was* he?

He heard the cat's human voice again: "Follow, follow."

It was coming from the other side of the room, where the tunnel continued. Truman looked over his shoulder. He wanted to go back to the house, to his bed, to Camille's snores. What good did his imagination ever do him? It got him in trouble during the day and it made it impossible to fall asleep at night. But, this very moment, he was imagining that there was something at the other end of the tunnel—something magical. He thought of the Breath World in his grandmother's tasting tale, and he could almost feel it calling to him from deep in the tunnel that lay in front of him. Was it real? And was this the way to it? He knew that if Camille were here she would say something like "Truman is afraid of the teacup ride at the amusement park. He'll turn around any second now and come home." But he wasn't turning around. He wasn't going home. He would follow the tunnel and see what was on the other end.

As he walked across the room, he stepped on something with his bare foot—something small and crisp, stiffer than a leaf, but not as hard as a bone. He shuddered and closed his eyes. He didn't want to know what it was. He kept on going, and when he reached the mouth of the tunnel, he held tight to the snow globe and kept crawling forward.

The tunnel went on, and Truman wondered how long it was. What if it didn't *have* an ending? He started to feel confined, a little claustrophobic. Was the tunnel getting tighter?

Finally, he saw a distant light. He crawled faster. His hand patted the dirt until he found one root and then another and another. He climbed the roots as if they were a ladder. And when he popped his head out of the tunnel, he saw two cat eyes, peering at him from a small, dimly lit room.

But it was not a cat—or not completely—because, as it reached forward to help him from the hole, it offered its pale little *human* hand.

CHAPTER NINE

The Breath World?

Truman stood in the small, dimly lit room. Everything was blurry, as if the room were underwater. There were strange catlike creatures weaving around his ankles, sniffing at the hems of his pajama pants, nosing his bare feet. There had to be a hundred of them at least. He was looking for the cat who'd led him here, an indistinct, furred black form, but now he couldn't tell one from the next—and these obviously weren't just cats. The creatures padded around on their back paws and human hands, and when they looked at Truman, they seemed to understand more than a cat would, though he wasn't sure what made him think that, exactly. They were all making soft mewling noises in the backs of their throats.

Truman looked around at the room. A potbelly stove, a tiny stone sink, cupboards, a square table with one lonely chair, a lantern sitting on the windowsill, a small bed stacked with quilts. He thought of Camille's snow globe with the little hut inside it and the woman peeking out the window. The room looked how he imagined the inside of the hut to be.

And the snow globe woman had cats on her shoulders. Could . . . could this be the same hut?

He looked over at one of the creatures, poised on the table, who'd picked up a piece of deep red fruit the size of a mandarin orange, and watched it peel the fruit open, just the way Truman would—first digging in a thumbnail and then pulling away the rind like bits of thick leather. Truman pushed his glasses up the bridge of his nose, hoping things would be clearer. But it didn't help. The animal cocked its head and stared at Truman as if they knew each other.

"Were you the one calling to me in the snow?" Truman asked finally.

The animal nodded and held the fruit up, offering him some.

"No, thanks," Truman said, not sure what to make of any of this. "Are you all cats?"

The mewler nibbled the fruit in its hands. "Mewlersss," it hissed, and the others echoed, "Mewlersss, mewlersss, mewlersss . . ."

"Mewlers?" Truman said, trying the word out. Could these mewlers be the kind of creatures that were kicked out of the Fixed World? If they were, then could this really be the Breath World itself, the one from his grandmother's story?

Behind the potbelly stove there were three mewlers knitting. Each had a ball of blue yarn and needles. They seemed to be making woolen hats.

"Hey," Truman said to the mewler eating the fruit, "my grandmother has one of those hats."

"Hatsss, hatsss," one of the knitting mewlers hissed,

and the other knitting mewlers repeated, "Hatsss, hatsss, hatsss . . ."

Just then, Truman heard a buzz, and three large flying bugs zipped past his face. Their wings sounded electric. One of the mewlers leapt from the table onto Truman's shoulder, trying to swipe at the bugs in midair. Instead the mewler hit Truman's glasses and sent them flying across the room. Truman groaned, but when he looked around, everything came into sharp focus—without his glasses on.

He was stunned. He took a moment to drink in the room with real clarity. But then another mewler leapt right on top of the snow globe in Truman's arms.

"Hey!" Truman said. "Watch out!" He stumbled backward and accidentally stepped on a paw. That mewler let out a violent screech and the others hissed, arching their backs.

"Sorry!" Truman said, inching back toward the tunnel. Maybe these creatures were kicked out of the Fixed World for a very good reason. Maybe they hated humans. "I think I should go home now. I'm not supposed to be here."

Then, from the other side of the room, there was a loud snort. "Who is it? Back again? Not this time!" The bed that Truman had thought was covered with quilts actually had just one quilt, covering a small, pudgy woman who was now rustling awake. She grabbed a rolling pin from under the pillow. "Listen here! I'm armed! And me mewlers are set to attack!" She waved the rolling pin blindly in the air.

The mewlers, taking their cue from her, became aggressive. They started grabbing Truman's legs, their claws digging through his pajama pants into his skin. He toppled over and they pounced on him. "Stop it!" he shouted. "Get off of me!"

"Where's Praddle? Is she home yet? Praddle?" the old woman was calling. Was this the mewler who'd led him to this terrifying place? "Who is it, mewlers? Who is here? Another thief?" And then Truman felt a hand reach into the pile of mewlers and pull him up by his pajama top.

For a brief moment, he was face to face with the old woman. She stared at him with her large eyes, one of which was a shocking bright blue and the other shiny and black—not an eye at all, really. It was more like a large, shiny black pearl!

And then Truman, gripping his snow globe with both arms, let out a scream—so sharp and high and sudden that it surprised even him. The old woman was shocked too, so much so that her hand sprang open, releasing Truman, and the mewlers all reared back.

Just as Truman scrambled to his feet, one mewler jumped and landed on his back. He had no time to shake it off. He hurled himself toward the front door, flung it open, and ran out into the dark, snowy night.

"Praddle!" the old woman was crying into the wind. "Praddle! Come back!"

CHAPTER TEN

The Rider's Cloak

With the swirling snow globe clutched to his chest and the creature on his back, Truman ran through the snow, dodging trees, jumping and stumbling over dips and roots. His heart was pounding in his ears. He could barely see in the dark. The snow was coming down fast. He kept running until he found the courage to glance behind him. No one was following—except the mewler hitching a ride on his shoulder.

"Get off!" Truman shouted breathlessly, and then he doubled over, his hands on his knees.

The mewler slipped off Truman's shoulder.

Truman looked at the mewler. "You're that cat that got me into this in the first place. Aren't you?"

"Mewlerrr," she said.

"Your name's Praddle, right?"

Praddle nodded.

Truman sat down on a rock, set the snow globe by his side, and rubbed his icy feet with his hands. "Well, Praddle, any idea on how to get me *out* of this?"

Praddle wrung her hands and shrugged.

The wind whipped Truman's hair and ruffled Praddle's shiny fur. Truman closed his eyes and tears slid from the corners. And when he closed his eyes, he saw the image of two eyes—one blue, one a black pearl. "Was that woman Swelda's sister?" Truman whispered. "Ickbee?"

"Yesss!" Praddle hissed.

"Why did she want to kill me?" Truman cried.

"She wasss being sssafe!" Praddle hissed.

"Really?" Truman snorted. "She was about to bludgeon me with a rolling pin!"

"She'sss been waiting for you!"

"She could have shown more hospitality," Truman said.

"You should go back to herrr!"

"I'm not going back there. No way." But where *was* he going? It was dark and cold and snowing. "I'll probably get frostbite and have to get my nose amputated," he muttered. He thought about Camille and wished she were with him. She'd know what to do. She'd read enough books about disasters to know something about how to survive.

Praddle hopped on a log, pointed downhill, and mewled in that partly human way she had back in Swelda's yard.

Truman shook his head. "I'm not falling for that again!"

Praddle hopped down and tugged at the leg of his pajamas, then pointed and mewled louder.

"This better be good."

Praddle pointed again, and Truman could see that there was a break in the trees. They were on a mountain. He walked to the log, climbed on top of it, and peered down into a valley. There he saw lights, lots of them, all clumped together. "A city!" he exclaimed. "Maybe I could get help there. Maybe someone knows how to help me back." But then he noticed how very far away the city was—through trees and across meadows, along a river. "It's too far," he said tiredly. "I'll never make it tonight. I'll freeze to death."

Praddle hopped up and down on the log, mewling, and then climbed off the log and slipped into its rotted-out center.

Truman knelt down at the mouth of the log and stared inside.

"Warmmm, warmmm," Praddle purred.

"Are you saying we could sleep in there?" Truman asked. "I'd get claustrophobic. Plus, we couldn't both be in there at the same time. I'm allergic to pet dander, and—"

"Shhh!" Praddle whispered, her finger held to her lips.

Truman heard a ruffle of feathers overhead. *Grossbeak?* he thought for a second. But then he looked up and saw a flock of strange birds soaring through the sky. The flock passed in and out of the fog, through the snow. The birds had bloodred hoods, long gawky necks, and hooked ivory beaks. Large talons hung under their meaty feathered ribs, and in their talons they carried round metal cages. The cages had creatures in them— Truman couldn't make out what they were. He saw hands gripping the bars, but also snouts and muzzles wedged between the bars, glimpses of fur and feathers and scales.

"What are those birds?" Truman whispered.

"Vulturesss," Praddle hissed.

One vulture, which had a tufted white back, didn't have a cage in its grip. It was skirting the edges of the flock. Suddenly it dipped closer to the ground, and Truman could see that what he'd thought was a tuft on its back wasn't one at all. It was a small person wearing a long iridescent robe, and he—or she—was riding the bird like a horse, but without a saddle or reins, handfuls of feathers in each fist. As the bird passed, Truman saw a long curved sword.

"Who is that?" Truman asked.

Praddle stared and shook her head. She didn't know.

As if the rider had heard Truman, the bird reared and turned back, circling toward the valley and the fallen tree where Truman stood, his breath caught in his throat.

Praddle mewled, and then darted into the hollow log.

Truman quickly dropped to the ground, grabbed his snow globe, and shimmied into the log where Praddle was now curled up in a tight, shivering ball. The vulture dipped so low that Truman could hear the ruffling of its wings. It landed right in front of the log.

Truman saw the bird's scaly talons and then the small leather boots of its rider and the hem of the rider's robe, which twitched and wriggled. The robe was alive, made of shimmering white bugs with delicate wings. They looked like pale, glistening locusts. Each summer, Truman saw locusts on the ground in his neighborhood, tapping at the dirt and cement. They were loud at night, trilling in the trees. But it was winter now. And why would anyone want a robe made out of bugs?

Did the rider know that Truman was there? Truman and Praddle were silent, barely breathing. The rider pulled out a sword, paced in one direction and then the other, and then the pair of boots—very small black boots—stopped right at the mouth of the log. Truman was afraid that the rider would be able to hear his heart, which sounded to Truman like a drum.

The rider's robe started to twitch and flutter as if the locusts were impatient to leave. Truman peered from the log and watched one of the bugs spread its wings in a quick flutter. And when the wings lifted, Truman saw the dainty body of a tiny person—not the body of a bug at all. A fairy-sized person. She turned her head, and Truman saw the profile of her quizzical little face.

The robe itself let out a rising, chirruping cry.

"Hushhh!" the rider hissed.

The bugs fell silent.

Then the rider climbed back atop the bird, and the bird took its great loping steps, raised its great wings, and flew up into the sky.

Truman held the snow globe to his chest and gave a sigh.

"Bewarrre," Praddle mewled.

"Who was it?" Truman asked.

Praddle shivered. "Sssomeone to fearrr."

"The robe," he said. "It looked like it was made out of locusts, but one of the locusts had a face."

"They all have facesss," Praddle hissed. "Locussst fairiesss."

Truman felt Praddle's warm fur on his feet. It was dark in the log, but snug and safe. Each time Truman closed his eyes, the rider's sword flashed in his mind. He wished his father were here. He wanted to hear the song his father sang to them every night, and so he sang it, ever so softly, under his breath:

"Sleep, slumber, sweet slumber ba-ru.
Sleepy-seed, sleepy-seed, dew.
Snug cover and pillow, hear the hush of the willow
And I will stand dream watch over you."

He sang it again and again until, with crunchy leaves for a pillow, he finally fell asleep.

CHAPTER ELEVEN

Wild Browsenberries

When Truman tried to roll over and couldn't, he remembered that he'd spent the night inside a log. He opened his eyes and blinked at the bright day. The world was miraculously clear and crisp and in focus. Truman had always woken up to a blurry world. He'd always had to reach for his glasses on his bedside table and slip them on before he could make anything out. But right now, he was looking out of the mouth of the hollow log at the shiny black fur of Praddle's coat, at the snow outside, at the ghostly outlines of trees against a cloudy sky. He didn't understand it, but he was ecstatic.

Truman crawled out into the bright sun and stood up. "I can see!" he told Praddle. The ground was layered in white. It was cold, but the snow had stopped. He hopped up on the log and looked down into the valley again. The fog had climbed higher up the mountain, and Truman gazed down at the miniature-looking houses and buildings, the crisscrossing streets. There was a river that wound through the outskirts, and it was dotted with boats and barges. And farther out of town, there were farms—white-blanketed pastures and fields, staked with fence posts.

For a moment it seemed that he could be looking at a valley in the Fixed World. His parents had once taken them to the Blue Ridge Mountains, and this wasn't all that different. He knew, of course, that he'd climbed through a tunnel into a strange world. But had he *imagined* vultures carrying creatures in cages, the old woman with the black pearl eye? And the mewlers—maybe they hadn't had human hands at all.

Truman felt a tug on the leg of his pajamas, and there was Praddle. She was holding a jacket and a pair of slippers, both woven from long, thick pointy leaves—holding them with her human hands.

"Mewl-mewl," she said.

And then it hit Truman that he was really here in the Breath World, lost and cold and now hungry too, and Praddle was his only friend. "Are these for me?"

She nodded.

He took the jacket and tried it on. It felt a little stiff and the leaves tickled his arms through his pajama top at first. But the jacket was woven so tightly that it blocked the wind. "Thank you, Praddle!"

She smiled and shrugged.

He slid his feet into the slippers. They fit perfectly and were warm and dry.

"How did you make all of this?"

Praddle fiddled with her hands as if to say *Like this!*

She scurried to some nearby bushes and started plucking berries.

"Breakfast?" Truman asked.

Praddle nodded.

The berries looked like little fuzzy moons. "Browsen-berries," he said. "I'm usually allergic to berries, but . . ." Truman wanted to test a theory. What if this really was the Breath World and the Breath World really was Swelda's home-land, and she really did import all of her foods from this world, and, for whatever reasons, Truman wasn't allergic to things here? Only one way to know. He popped a browsenberry into his mouth, and as soon as he bit into it and the berry burst and his mouth filled with its tart juice, he remembered, vividly, a tiny bit of the tasting tale: *All those magical creatures—the ones you see now only in dreams and stories—used to walk among us.* He knew in an instant that this was exactly the thing he'd been tasting when Swelda said those words.

"Praddle," Truman said, "have you ever been told a tast-ing tale?"

She smiled and nodded quickly.

"Okay, then later, after you hear a tasting tale, if you eat something that was served to you when you were being told that tale, do you remember it exactly?"

Praddle nibbled her berries and gave a nod.

Truman ate another handful of berries and Swelda's words echoed again in his mind: *All those magical creatures— the ones you see now only in dreams and stories—used to walk among us.* . . .

"Praddle," Truman began, "do . . . do you have dragons around here?"

"Dragonsss?"

"You know, lizardlike creatures with small wings and sometimes horns and long tails who breathe fire?"

"Oh, fire-breathersss. Yesss."

Truman felt a prickle of fear. "What about unicorns? Like deer but they only have one horn?"

"One-horned boundersss," she said. "Of courssse."

"Mermaids? Half woman, half fish?"

"Bogpeople," she said. "Very muddy."

"Elves? You know, little people?"

"Yesss, urfsss."

"What about centaurs? Half horse, half human?"

Looking a little tired of all the questions, she just sighed and spread her arms out wide in one big swooping gesture that Truman took to mean, *We have them all!*

Truman shook his head. "It's hard to believe," he said. He felt scared and hopeful, both at once. *You come from the long line*—that was what his grandmother had said. Did that long line go all the way back to this place? Was his father here, somewhere? Could he find him?

Praddle tapped the snow globe. "Thisss wasss Ickbee'sss."

"Oh, right," Truman said, remembering that Swelda had written that in her note. "It's kind of a strange gift. It has a man in it who's just been stabbed. It's a little morbid. Not your regular Christmas tree and snowman. See?" He pointed to the scene and ate some more berries. *All those magical creatures—the ones you see now only in dreams and stories—used to walk among us.*

Praddle leaned in and then looked up at him, confused. She shook her head.

"What is it?" Truman asked.

Praddle tapped the snow globe again.

He lifted it up and looked more closely. The snow was settling in a small, dark, cluttered room with lots of velvety drapes—what seemed to be a museum. There were taxidermied creatures wall-mounted or standing midgrowl and midclaw or, in the case of winged creatures, strung from the ceiling midflight. There were lots of variations—horns, beaks, thorny tails, ridged backs, tightly curled tusks, human-looking gazes. There was even a full-sized fire-breather, its wings unfurled, its fangs bared.

There was also a wall-mounted display of weaponry— from crude spears to slick blades so shiny they reflected like mirrors.

There was something about the creatures—their terrified eyes, their yowling mouths. These weren't fake stuffed creatures, like Swelda's vulture. These animals had once lived, had been hunted down, and now were dead.

In one corner he saw a finger—a solitary index finger with a spiral ring sitting just below the knuckle—preserved in a jar. *What happened to the rest of him?* Truman wondered, with a shudder.

"This can't be right," Truman said, peering at the globe. "Yesterday, there was a man who'd been stabbed and a woman wearing a cloak with a big hood. It was as clear as anything, but now . . ."

Just then a tiny door opened. A small billowy cloud of locust fairies appeared—like a swirl of snow themselves— and a boy was shoved into the room, his ankles bound, his hands tied behind his back, his mouth gagged. The bindings weren't regular cloth, though. They seemed to be made of thousands of fine silken threads. The boy fell forward and lay on the floor. The locust fairies disappeared. The door slammed shut. The boy was now all alone.

Truman turned the globe this way and that, staring at the boy inside. The boy looked to be about Truman's age, and he had brown hair and green eyes, like Truman. In fact, he looked a lot like Truman in many ways. But he wasn't Truman.

The strangest thing was that no matter how Truman turned the globe in his hands, it seemed as if the boy was staring at him. And his expression surprised Truman. The boy wasn't terrified, as Truman would have been, bound up and locked in a miserable museum. No. This boy seemed re-signed to it. He hadn't given up, exactly, but it was as if he'd been expecting it. He stared at Truman with tenderness, and now and then a little flash of warning. *Be careful*, the boy seemed to be saying. *It's going to be okay. Don't be scared. But be careful.*

Truman shut his eyes, but he felt that the boy in the globe could still see him. And Truman knew, somehow, that he had to find the boy and help him.

"What does this mean?" Truman asked Praddle

"Ickbee'sss," Praddle said. "Sssafe at Ickbee'sss. Go back?"

"Safe? With a woman who wants to beat me with a rolling pin?"

"Missstake," Praddle hissed. "Her hut iss sssafe!"

"I don't want to be safe," Truman said, and this surprised him. Truman Cragmeal had spent his life wanting to be safe. He was still scared—terrified, in fact, at the prospect of head-ing into a strange city in this strange world—but there was some new part of himself that was emerging. Or was it that a sleeping part of himself was waking up, like an arm that falls asleep and feels dead but then slowly tingles back to life? "I'm going to the city to see what I can figure out. Where there are people, there have to be some answers." He stood up. "Are you coming?"

Praddle nodded.

CHAPTER TWELVE

The Worlds Are at Stake!

Camille was woken up by the sound of a loud pop, like a tire exploding or a car backfiring or a gunshot. She sat upright in bed. The room was dark except for a few little rays of light slipping between the boards that covered the windows. She said, "Truman! Did you hear that?" But then she looked over at his bed.

He was gone.

And then she remembered what Swelda had said about being early risers. *Golfers!* she said to herself. The pops were golf balls hitting the house. Truman was a light sleeper. The golf balls had probably already woken him up, she figured.

She slipped out of bed—her feet on the cold floor—and looked out through one of the cracks between the boards.

There was a light dusting of snow on the ground, but this didn't stop the hearty golfers—and neither did the fog. Two of them were out there on the green. The fog was so dense that Camille could see only their brightly colored pants and the heads of their golf clubs. They were trying to tap their

balls—bright orange ones to stand out against the snow—
into the little cup.

The snow reminded Camille of the snow globes. She
walked to the bedside table. Truman had taken his with him.
And hers? She forgot for a moment she'd fallen asleep holding it. It was lost in the bedcovers. She patted the quilt until
she found the hard glass ball. She pulled it out and gave it a
shake, wanting to see the snow swirl around the little mud
hut again. As the snow churned, the scene disappeared in the
white. Camille watched the snow settle slowly, and as it did,
a new scene appeared: a sloping hill covered with trees, their
limbs weighted with snow. A path wound through the forest,
and in the snow on the path there were footprints. Then she
turned the globe a little and saw a figure between the trees.

She turned the globe again, trying to get a closer look. It
was a boy in a big fur hat and a jacket made of leaves.

She peered closer.

It wasn't a boy in a big fur hat. It was a boy wearing a
wide-eyed cat on his head.

A boy in blue pajama bottoms.

"Truman," Camille whispered. The water in the globe
was trembling, because her hands were trembling.

Just then there was a knock on the bedroom door. "It's
time!" her grandmother's voice rang out. "The boy has gone
through to the other side!"

"Other side?" Camille echoed.

"And she's lost him! Already! May I come in?"

"Yes," Camille said, her voice dry in her throat.

The door swung open. There stood her grandmother,

dressed for the day in jeans, a sweater, and her white sneakers. She was wearing the blue woolen hat. "Your brother!" she said. "He's lost!"

"Who lost him? How?"

"Well, my dingbat sister, of course. Let him run off!"

Camille looked at her grandmother, and her grandmother stared back at her with her one good eye.

"Truman's gone *where?*" Camille asked.

"The Breath World, my dear! Aren't you listening?" she said, and then she clapped. "Hurry up! Get dressed, pack a small bag, and bring the snow globe. You'll need it. The worlds are at stake!"

CHAPTER THIRTEEN

Into the City of Creatures

The path through the forest was covered with small stones, some of which were crusted in ice and had become slick. Burrs and nettles lined the path. Whenever Truman slipped, the nettles snagged his flannel pajama pants and the burrs gripped on like Velcro. Praddle was curled on his head, keeping it warm, but every time he slid one way or the other, she had to scramble to keep her roost.

It didn't help that Truman was easily distracted by all of the creatures. They were everywhere, fluttering, twittering, rustling in the underbrush, howling in the distance. Truman would catch glimpses of them scurrying up a tree or peering at him from a knothole. He could only make out eyes, the swish of a tail, a bit of beak.

Once he heard a strange clacking noise coming from the dense forest.

"What's that?" he whispered to Praddle. "Did you hear something?"

Praddle swiveled her head in the direction of the noise. "There," she whispered.

Truman put his hand on a tree trunk to steady himself and then peered through the trees into a glade. There he saw unicorns—two of them. They looked somewhat young, but each had a brilliant twisted horn, and they were fighting with each other. They didn't seem violent, though. It was as if they were only practicing. Their coats were a dusty brown, their ears perked. They looked majestic.

"They're beautiful," Truman said. But when he took another step, his foot snapped a twig. The unicorns froze, then bounded deeper into the forest.

Eventually the trees thinned, and Truman and Praddle came to open farmland. Truman saw a herd of what seemed to be cattle up ahead. But as he and Praddle made their way down the dirt road closer to the herd, Truman noticed that the grazing animals had plumes of smoke swirling above their heads. It couldn't just be their breath in the cold air. The smoke was thick. It chugged up from their mouths like smoke from old trains. That was when he started to be able to make out the spiky ridges on their backs. One lifted its head and then sat back on its haunches and stretched, unfolding a pair of restless wings. A bell on its neck gave a hollow *tock-tock*, and then the creature settled back down to grazing.

"Those aren't cows at all!" Truman said.

"Herrrd of domesticated fire-breathersss," Praddle explained, as if this were the most ordinary thing of all.

The houses grew closer together. Shops sprang up, and soon Truman and Praddle found themselves in the thick of the city. Truman held the snow globe in one arm and Praddle in the other, and they jostled through an open-air market. Stalls were set up on either side of the narrow road. An eight-foot giant hawked barrels of mead. A spindly man with only one eye—in the center of his forehead—was announcing a new line of pickled cabbage. A beast that looked like a living gargoyle—monkeyish, with fangs, and dragonlike too, with scaly skin—was offering remedies for toothache and gout. A diminutive centaur blacksmith had a line of hoofed creatures, snorting impatiently, awaiting new horseshoes.

Truman and Praddle bustled by the opening of a large tent. Loud shouting, singing, wheezy accordions playing offbeat polkas, and the noisy din of bongos billowed out from its flaps. "Ruckusss tentsss," Praddle hissed.

"What's inside of them?" Truman asked, trying to get a peek.

"Ruckusesss!"

There was an electrified air to the city. Truman loved the oddness of it all—the noises, the strange smells, the creatures. He felt as if he were being pushed along by a strong current. Everyone seemed to be heading into the city, and no one was moving against the tide—except for a company of large hairy spiders. Truman spotted them hustling along the gutter in a long, tidy row.

He stopped and pointed them out to Praddle. "What are they doing?"

"Don't point!" one of the spiders scolded. "Didn't your mother tell you it ain't polite?"

"Sorry," Truman said. "Where are you all headed?"

"Tired of being treated like dirt," the spider said. "There's jobs for us. Good jobs, too, from what we hear. Up in the highlands. The lightning wing-beaters is already working, and the fire-breather flies."

"Good luck," Truman said, marveling over having conducted his first actual conversation with a spider.

The spider gave him a nasty look. "And good riddance!"

Truman wasn't sure what to make of that. He backed away from the angry spider and joined the crowd again. It wasn't long before he noticed a cage and, locked inside it, a horned man wearing a tweed suit and a blue necktie. The cage sat in front of a spice shop. It was the same kind of cage he'd seen the vultures carrying through the snowy sky the night before. Truman stopped in his tracks.

Attached to the cage by wire was a sign: HORNED BEAST. THREAT TO OUR GOODNESS. SPY. BETRAYER. JARKMAN.

The man was staring off, unaware of Truman.

"Did he do something really wrong?" Truman asked Praddle.

Praddle shook her head. "He disssagreed . . . ," she hissed.

"With . . . ?"

Praddle swiveled her head, checking all directions, and then she whispered, "Official Affairsss."

Truman looked around and saw other cages—between the hawkers' carts and tents, sitting on the ground, swaying heavily from lampposts. All were marked "Property of the Office of Official Affairs." He read a few of the signs: BAN- SHEE. MIXED BREED OF MONKEY-BIRD. URF. KNURL. Most of them also ended with JARKMAN.

Now Truman also saw that there were posters tacked to the sides of buildings and tents. Above the slogan US VERSUS THEM! THE DIFFERENCE IS SIMPLE! they all showed a picture of a man with a hawk's beak who had plumage sticking out around the collar of his shirt and the sleeves of his suit jacket.

The feathered man stuck out his little dimpled chin and looked squinty-eyed. Two protruding ears completed the unsettling image.

Truman was sick to his stomach. "What does it all mean? I don't understand."

Praddle shook her head and put a hand over her mouth. She couldn't talk about it, not here.

All of a sudden, Truman felt disoriented. "Maybe we should try to go back, up the mountain. Maybe I can sneak into the hut and find the hole and go back to Swelda's."

But Praddle wasn't paying attention. She climbed up Truman's arm and sat tall on his shoulder.

"Praddle," he said. "Are you listening? This city's too big. We'll never find the boy in the snow globe."

Praddle mewled.

"What is it?"

She pointed into the crowded streets.

"What is it?" Truman said again.

"Mewl-mewl!" she cried.

And then Truman spotted it too. A blue woolen hat on a man's head. An ugly blue woolen hat that could have been knit by mewlers. Truman raced into the crowd, against the flow of traffic. He dipped down, dodging in and out among people and their big woven baskets. He kept an eye on the hat. It bobbed along through the crowd.

Truman knocked into someone's basket.

"Watch out!" a well-dressed fawn bleated, trying to regain his balance on his hooves.

"Sorry," Truman said.

At one point, Truman got down on his knees and, clutching the snow globe in one arm, slipped behind the stalls to try to gain on the man in the hat. But he was blocked by an ogre.

"Get out of here!" the ogre yelled. "Are you some kind of thief?"

"No, no!" Truman said. "I'm not a thief!"

The ogre reached out to grab Truman but he dipped down and crawled back out into the street.

He hopped up and down to see the hat in the sea of creatures. He caught glimpses of one odd creature after another. They were a blur of claws, hands, horns, pudgy noses and snouts, feathers, and furry forearms. It was like a dream, but the kind of dream that seems like a stranger but almost truer version of home.

Praddle pointed again. "Mewl!"

Truman saw the tip of the hat—just the faintest bit of blue. The man had stopped. He was standing under a sign that read EDWELL'S HOPS AND CHOPS HOUSE. He was gazing through the plate glass window.

"Hurrry," Praddle purred urgently.

Truman hid down the alley next to a store called Idgit's Inkhorn and Plume Shop. "What will I say? *Where did you get that hat?* I don't know what the hat even means." Truman peered around the corner at the man in the blue hat, getting a good look at him for the first time. "Wait," Truman said. "I know that man!"

It was the man who'd been stabbed in the first scene that Truman had seen in his snow globe—the man on the ground, blood spreading across his white shirt. But his shirt was white now, not stained at all. He was fine.

Truman looked at the snow globe. "Does it make things up?" Truman asked Praddle. "How does it work?"

"Futurrre, passst, presssent. They'rrre all ssswirrrled, like sssnow."

Truman stared at Praddle and then at the snow globe. "If it was telling the future, then I might be able to save him." He paused. "Who is he, Praddle?"

"He'sss one of usss."

Truman decided to take another look. He moved one step beyond the corner of the building and heard a sharp squeak.

"Hey, there! Watch it, you giant galumph!"

Truman looked down and saw a mouse wearing a red vest and a plaid scarf. The mouse had a rolled-up piece of paper in his fist, and he shook it at Truman.

Praddle bared her teeth.

"Sorry," Truman said, retreating to his spot in the alley, with his back against the wall.

"You should all be shrunk! Oversized idiots," the mouse muttered, and then scurried on.

CHAPTER FOURTEEN

Magical Afflictions

Swelda ushered Camille toward the front door. They both stepped over a chunk of plaster that had fallen from the ceiling and lay in a dusty heap. "Oh my!" she said under her breath. "It's beginning to self-destruct!"

"What's self-destructing?" Camille asked.

Swelda didn't answer. "Here's a sack lunch," she said. She turned Camille around, unzipped her backpack, and stuck a brown paper bag inside. "Keep track of the snow globe, of course. It will be of great use!"

Camille was still a little dazed. "I saw Truman inside it."

"What was he up to?"

"He was walking through a forest."

"Oh drat!"

"And last night there was a woman peeking out of a little house that seemed covered with roots and vines."

"My sister's house, yes. That's where you're off to now." Swelda shoved Camille toward the door.

"But why do things change in the snow globe?"

"Life changes, doesn't it?"

"Is it showing me things going on somewhere else right now, or is it predicting things?"

"Yes, both, and sometimes you look inside and can see the past. These three snow globes are nimble like that. When you least expect, they will sting you with a memory. . . ." Her voice drifted off as if she had some memories she'd rather not be stung by again.

"I hate to interrupt you, deep in thought like that, but how do I *get* to the Breath World?" Camille said, impatient.

"Ah, yes! Go out into the yard, around back, to the cellar. There you'll find the passageway. Follow it to the Breath World. My sister will be waiting."

"Your twin sister? The one in the picture?"

"Yes. Ickbee is her name. There is more to the tasting tale, but I'll let her tell it." She stood up straight, closed her eye, and smiled. "Yes, yes, she'll be ready for you. I see her dithering around, preparing your arrival."

"But why is all of this happening now?" Camille asked.

"Didn't I tell you already?"

Camille shook her head.

"The Ever Breath was protected by an enchantment cast on Ickbee's house and mine," Swelda whispered. "But someone broke the enchantment and the Ever Breath is gone. Have you noticed that this house is about to fall in?"

Camille glanced around. "Well, I didn't want to say anything, but—"

"That's why your father went to the Breath World. To find the Ever Breath. He will need you two there, to help return the Ever Breath to its rightful place." And then she snapped her fingers over her head. "Oh, yes. I almost forgot," she said. She walked quickly to the bookcase, pulled out a heavy tome, and took out a small photograph. She handed it to Camille. "You might need this."

It was a picture of a boy about Camille's age. "Who is it?"

"It's your father when he was twelve years old. We haven't had any communication from him for a few days. He's been in dangerous territory, trying to get the Ever Breath back. I'm sure he'll be fine. But when you see him again, this is the person you'll be looking at in the Breath World. Your father as a boy."

Startled, Camille looked up at Swelda. "What do you mean?"

"We all have our magical afflictions."

"Magical afflictions?"

"Your father is a forever child. He could have lived in the Breath World and stayed a boy forever. But he chose not to."

Camille held the photograph and stared at the image of her father. He looked a little like Truman, actually. She felt as if the fog outside had moved into her head. She felt dazed and scared. "But Truman and I aren't magical," she said slowly.

"Ah, but you come from the long line!"

"You said that before but we didn't get it. The long line of what?"

"Gramarye," Swelda whispered. "It's an ancient term. Do you think that when the magical creatures were separated and cast out—the Exodus, as we say—do you think that those who could perform a bit of magic, those who could both enchant and curse, were allowed to stay here?"

"I guess not," Camille said.

"You are of the Breath World, yes, a magical creature and one who can do some magic. Your magical afflictions just haven't shown up yet, not in full."

"I'm going to get magically afflicted. Is that what you're saying? I mean, I knew we were kind of dysfunctional, but *afflicted*?"

"It's part of growing up in this family."

"Or part of *not* growing up," Camille said, shaking her father's photograph.

"I guess that's true, in some cases."

Camille put the photograph in the zippered pouch of her backpack and then looked down at her shoes. "I'm not sure I'm really the one you want doing this. I mean, I'm not as tough as I look."

"You're exactly the one. No one else in the worlds will do." Swelda then took off her blue woolen hat and put it on Camille's head. "Keep this with you. That way they'll know you're one of us. Ickbee will answer any other questions."

Swelda pulled Camille's coat off of the hall tree. The tree—it was such a strange thing. It couldn't really be alive, surviving there in the dark house. Camille reached out quickly and touched its bark. It was as rough and real as that of any tree she'd ever touched. The tree seemed sickly, but alive. Very much so.

"Does this tree blossom in the spring?" Camille blurted out as she put on her coat.

"Of course! Beautiful pink blossoms. They carpet the hall for weeks! And clog the vacuum cleaner!" But then Swelda's face grew serious and she patted the tree's trunk. "I hope it blossoms this year!" She then turned to Camille and gave her a quick hug. "Go quickly now. No time to waste."

With a backward glance at the tree, Camille went to the front door and twisted the knob—which fell off in her hand. "Here," she said, and handed it to her grandmother.

"Thanks," Swelda said. She pushed open the front door and Camille stepped into the bright snowy world.

CHAPTER FIFTEEN

King of the Jarkmen

The next time Truman rounded the corner to catch up with the young man in the blue woolen hat, he smacked right into a bony chest and fell backward onto the ground. Praddle screeched, and Truman bobbled the snow globe. It nearly slipped from his hands.

"So sorry!" a voice from above said.

Truman looked up and there, standing over him, was the man in the blue woolen hat. He was younger than Truman had thought—only in his late teens or maybe his early twenties.

"Are you okay?" the young man asked. "Nearly broke that, didn't you?" He extended his hand. Truman took it, and the young man helped him to his feet.

The man pulled his thin coat in tight to his ribs and yanked the blue wool hat down over his ears. "How's the mewler?" he asked.

Truman brushed off Praddle's fur and scooped her up. "She's okay, I think."

"Good to hear. All right, then. Glad all's well. Have a

good day." And with that, the young man headed on down the road.

"Wait!" Truman called. "Hold on!" The young man was striding away quickly. Truman ran to catch up. "Sir," he said. "Um, excuse me!"

The young man turned around. He was very thin—so thin he'd had to tighten his belt to the last notch to keep his baggy woolen pants up. He had brown eyes—gentle eyes, really—and a nervous smile.

"Where are you going?" Truman asked.

"For a walk around the block. I've got a dinner appointment at Edwell's, but I'm early."

So it was almost dinnertime. Truman hadn't realized how long it had taken to get down the mountain. No wonder he was hungry again. "Can I walk with you? I've got a few questions."

The young man looked over his shoulder. "I don't like questions," he said. "They seem to always want answers."

"Just a few."

He hesitated. "What's your name?"

"Truman. And this is Praddle."

"I'm Artwhip," the young man said, and then a locust fairy orbited his head. "Dang locust fairies!" he exclaimed, waving his hand around. "They can't seem to get enough of me!"

The locust fairy buzzed Truman, who pivoted and ducked. "They like me too," Truman said.

"So we have something in common." Artwhip cast his eyes over the crowd, then gave a stiff nod. "Okay, kid. Come on."

Truman tried to match the young man's stride. "Where did you get that hat?" he asked.

They were walking down an alley, a shortcut back to the open-air market. The alley was dark. Strung overhead were carpets being aired, and they batted about in the cold wind, blocking Truman's view.

"This? It's just a present from my mother. Well, I think it's from my mother. My landlady gave me the package this morning. It came with a note, but the landlady spilt chatter-broth tea all over the note while snooping, most likely." He paused. "Well, that's not fair, I guess. She's only got paws, though, so she's clumsy like that."

"Oh," Truman said, thinking that paws for hands would be a difficult way to go through life. "Does your mother knit?"

Artwhip shrugged. They'd come to the end of the alley and now moved into the crowded market. "Don't all mothers knit?" He looked at the boy. "I thought you were going to ask me for money. I thought, well, in those strange clothes, the homemade jacket and shoes . . . Look, do you just want the hat? The weatherspy is predicting more snow." He stopped and peered up at the sky.

Truman looked up too. "I don't want the hat," he said. "It's just that . . . I've seen you before."

"You have?"

"I think I've seen a future version of you."

Artwhip stopped and stared at Truman and gave a quick laugh. "You're a futurist, then?"

"A futurist?" People rushed by them. The hawkers were all shouting at the same time. Someone in an apartment overhead was practicing scales on a squeaky horn. "Something bad is going to happen," Truman said.

This seemed to get the young man's attention. "To me?"

"Yes," Truman said. "I think it was you. I'm almost positive."

Artwhip walked up to a news peddler—a fish-man with fluttery gills on his cheeks and neck, watery eyes, and a drooped, whiskered face. "Do you know what time it is?" Artwhip asked the peddler.

"Did you see the latest edition?" the peddler shouted at him, holding up a copy of a newspaper called *The Official Facts, Presented to You Daily by the Office of Official Affairs*. The man's booth had one of the posters on it: the tough feathered man with the hawk's beak glaring above the slogan US VERSUS THEM! THE DIFFERENCE IS SIMPLE! "They just put this news on the streets!"

On the front page of the newspaper was a photograph of a boy with a weary expression but neatly combed hair—a cross between a mug shot and a school photograph. The boy looked familiar. Truman leaned in closer. The brown hair, the look in the boy's eyes—he was the boy that Truman had seen inside his snow globe. He was sure of it!

Artwhip read the headline aloud: "'Cragmeal, King of the Jarkmen, Public Enemy Number One.'"

"Cragmeal?" Truman said. That was his family's name! He leaned forward and started reading the news story.

Cragmeal, former King of the Jarkmen—a society of traitors that the Office of Official Affairs has officially dismantled—has been spotted in numerous locations.

A traitor to his own people, Cragmeal deserted

his post as king to live in the Fixed World. Now he is back to wreak havoc in our own land! He has been seen with blood-betakers, were-creatures, and other enemies of the Office.

"We intend to capture Cragmeal, once and for all. It is our sworn duty here at the Office to keep all of you safe!" declared Wilward Dobbler, President of the Office of Official Affairs this morning. . . .

Truman stared at the grainy photograph. Was it his father, as a boy? The boy bound in that awful museum and this boy, here, in the photograph? He felt breathless, the same way he'd felt when he fell into the cellar. It was like the beginning of an asthma attack. He reached for the inhaler he kept in his pocket, but of course he didn't have it. His inhaler was in the pocket of his jeans at Swelda's house, a world away.

Was his father a traitor, Public Enemy Number One? It wasn't possible. He glanced at Artwhip, who was leaning over him reading the article as quickly as he could. Truman wondered what would happen to him if the people here knew that Cragmeal was his father. And what did the article mean, "former King of the Jarkmen"? His father wasn't ever a king. He was the manager of three Taco Grills.

Praddle gave a hiss and tightened her grip on Truman's shoulder. She didn't like what she was reading either.

"They're gonna get'm, but good," the news peddler said,

and then he whispered to Artwhip, "What side do you stand on?"

Artwhip gave a little shake of his head. He wasn't saying a word. Truman had the feeling it was a dangerous question.

The peddler didn't wait for an answer anyway. He said loudly, "What kind of king was he anyways? Disloyal! A traitor to his people. Runnin' off like he did. And now he's back, lurking around, consorting with our enemies!" The news peddler's teeth were jagged and his words sounded wet. He splayed his hand over the article and leaned in close to Truman's face. "Stealing it with your eyes, are you? You don't get to read it for free!"

Both Truman and Artwhip stepped away quickly.

Truman remembered the tasting tale. He felt it stirring inside him. If the Ever Breath fell into the wrong hands, everything was in jeopardy. In the Fixed World, dreaming and imagining would end, and in the Breath World, imagination would take over in bad ways, with evil beasts rising up—a kind of self-destruction. Truman grabbed hold of Artwhip's sleeve.

Artwhip looked shaken. He gazed around as if disoriented. Sitting in a cage nearby was the man in the tweed suit from earlier. They'd circled the city and now were back in front of the spice shop.

The man in the tweed suit saw Artwhip's hat and sucked in his breath. Quickly, he rolled up his sleeves, revealing arms covered with blinking eyes. "The hat!" the man whispered. "The blue hat!"

Artwhip ran his hand along his hat and then looked at

Truman. He seemed tired and confused. "I've got to be going now," he said, and then he bowed politely and headed off.

"You can't leave me!" Truman cried, running after him.

Artwhip dipped beneath the paper lanterns bobbing in the gusts of wind and hurried back down a cut-through alley strung with carpets.

Truman followed. "Wait! You're going to get stabbed! I've seen it!"

"Stabbed? Me?" Artwhip said, over his shoulder. "Thanks for the warning. All the more reason for you to leave me alone."

"One more question," Truman shouted down the alley.

"No more questions!" Artwhip said.

Truman stopped running. He stood in the alley and shouted, "Is Cragmeal a traitor like the man said?"

Artwhip stopped in his tracks. He turned around and dipped under a strung-up carpet so that he and Truman were face to face. He looked at Truman, standing there, breathless, and whispered, "I still believe in Cragmeal. I've devoted myself to the cause." He lifted his shirt and revealed the hilt of a dagger—the feathered head of a snake, just like the one on the crest in Swelda's parlor, the one with the crown of feathers like Grossbeak's.

"What's that mean?" Truman asked.

"I'm a jarkman," Artwhip said. "A revolutionary."

Did this mean that Truman's *grandmother* was a revolutionary? "You're for Cragmeal?"

"He's my king, but I'm new." Artwhip balled up his fists and shoved them in his pockets. "I'm awaiting orders, but I think they've forgotten about me, or worse."

"Worse?"

"It's been twelve years since we had a king to lead the jarkmen. We've been losing members and faith. And then the news spread that Cragmeal was back." Artwhip shrugged, helpless. "But where is he now? Will the jarkmen believe people like the news peddler? That Cragmeal's a traitor? Maybe we're falling apart. Maybe there's no longer a chain of communication. Maybe so many of us are caged up that it's all over." His eyes were wide and watery. Truman hoped he wasn't going to cry. Truman felt like crying himself and he knew he couldn't. Not now. There was too much at stake.

He walked up close to Artwhip and whispered, "I think I know where Cragmeal is. Are there any museums in this world? Dark ones with stuffed creatures and chopped-off fingers in glass cases?"

Artwhip stared at him. "Chopped-off fingers?"

At that moment, bullhorn speakers crackled. Then they squawked one of their prerecorded warnings: *"The enemy may be among us! The threat level is five. We repeat, five. Please report any suspicious behavior. Turn in information about any suspected jarkmen. This message comes to you from the Office of Official Affairs."*

Artwhip and Truman looked up at the speakers, which were attached to the corner of the building at the end of the alley.

"What are they talking about?" Truman asked. The speakers were repeating the warning. Truman hated the crackle, the droning voice, the electrified nervousness.

"Five is the highest level, but it's always a level-five

warning. Why have levels if it's always set at the highest?" Artwhip said, shaking his head.

"What is the Office of Official Affairs?"

Artwhip blinked. "Where are you from? Up in the highlands? You don't know what the Office is?"

Truman shook his head.

"The Office of Official Affairs has divided all of us into the Officially Good and the Officially Evil, trying to make us believe that there are only two types of creatures. To protect the Officially Good, the Office has to do away with the Officially Evil."

"How can they tell the Officially Good from the Officially Evil?"

"Ah, well. It's simple." Artwhip raised his finger. "The Officially Good agree with the Office of Official Affairs, and the Officially Evil don't." He lowered his voice. "But the Office doesn't seem to have any real idea of what it means to be truly good—kind, brave, thoughtful. My father wants to achieve Official Goodness—to have his name, Archimeld P. Ostwiser, written on a folder, filed away in the Office of Official Affairs, with all of his important dates and distinctions and a wax seal pressed onto the documents so that he's good and he can prove it." He paused and took a deep breath. "The problem is that this desire to be Officially Good is the thing that allows my father to pass through the cage-lined streets and separate himself from the caged creatures. And that, Truman, is the most dangerous element of all! Do you understand?"

Truman nodded, but he wasn't sure he understood any of it.

Artwhip clapped Truman on the shoulder. "I haven't eaten anything but watery stew and old lard cakes for weeks. You're hungry too. Aren't you?"

Truman nodded again. He felt like he was starving, actually. He'd had nothing but berries all day.

"My father's in the restaurant around the corner right this moment. He's probably inspecting his teeth in the reflection on his cutlery. When I walk in there, he's going to tell me that I'm too skinny and I should get a real job in his department at the Office of Official Affairs so I can fatten up and live a normal life." Artwhip put his hands on his hips and let out a great sigh. He looked at Truman. "But if you're there, maybe it'll distract him a little."

"I can be very distracting," Truman said.

"Good, because they've got great food—fatty rinds of beef, broiled beet-nuts, stuffed mutton, bee ale, goose-egg chowder, potted cheeses, and chunks of sugar-crusted angel bread the size of my fist!"

Truman opened his mouth to tell him about all of his allergies, but then he closed it. Things were different in this world. "Thanks," he said. "I'd love to come."

"Okay, then," Artwhip said. "Bring the mewler too. The best thing about my father is that he always picks up the tab."

CHAPTER SIXTEEN

Magical Gifts

Camille remembered that the third step was missing. She jumped over the space and landed in the cellar, her hands clamped on her backpack's shoulder straps. She looked past the gears, tubes, and corks, the baskets of berries, searching for the passageway to the Breath World. There was no time to waste—Truman was lost and her father, just a boy now, was there too. They needed her.

After scanning the room, she squatted down. From there, she spied a hole in the wall—a hole with a faint dim glow.

It was too small to crawl into with the backpack on her back. She quickly reversed it so that it sat on her chest and pushed the globe off to the side a bit so that she wouldn't press on it too hard. Then she got down on all fours and pushed herself in. She crawled as swiftly as she could. The glowing jars of browsenberry wine lit her way. She thought of Truman. Lost in the woods? Lost in the Breath World? He was afraid of bullies and sidewalk cracks. How would he survive?

The passageway got tighter. She felt as if she could barely

breathe. The dirt was crumbling at the edges. She could feel the moist earth dampening the knees of her jeans. She started to wonder if her grandmother was crazy. Was any of this real? It would have felt like a dream, but the smell of the earth was too clear, the sound of the jostling snow globe inside the backpack too precise. She'd never dreamed in that kind of detail.

And then she came to a room with a branch reaching up into the shape of a gnarled and knotted hand—a hand holding nothing. The pinky was curled completely, as if it were broken and in need of a splint. She touched the rough bark, let her hand slip into the wooden hand. It was warm and strong.

There was something about the room that made her want to sit there and think about things. It felt like a place where you could come to some understanding. She didn't have time to linger, though. She walked toward the tunnel up ahead, and that was when she saw the little husks.

They were small and translucent, the kind she'd read about in stories of survivors who'd had to eat locusts. Locusts molted and left behind strange, alien-looking exoskeletons. There was a small pile of them—two dozen or more. Some were broken into shards; others were still intact. What were they doing here in this hidden room deep under the ground?

She heard a noise up ahead—almost like a howling wind.

Then there was banging—sharp, hard knocks. Five in a row, then a pause. Then four more, a pause, and then six bangs in a row.

She began crawling into the tunnel on the other side of the room, moving steadily until she saw light at the end—a golden light. She climbed up and out of the hole . . . into a tiny one-room hut. As soon as Camille stood up, she felt strange. Her eyesight was blurry and dim.

Was there dust in her eyes from the tunnel? She closed her eyes and then opened them again. The room was filled with blurry objects—a fat stove, a table and chair, ceiling-hung crockery, narrow cupboards. The walls, of mud and roots and vines, were twisting with shadows that weren't shadows at all. They were cats with human hands, walking everywhere—on the small bed, the counter, the table. And it was there, on the table, that she saw Truman's glasses, neatly folded. Her heart lurched in her chest. She rubbed her eyes, then took another look. Yes. They were his glasses, all right. It was proof. He'd really been here!

The banging was coming from an old woman wearing a wooly blue knit hat. She was holding a hammer and trying to wedge a thick branch into one of the room's saggy corners, using the branch as a tent pole. She seemed flustered, but strong. She was muttering wildly under her breath, through lips that were crimped around nails. The other corners of the room were propped up by sticks already, but one of the sticks had snapped in half just above the sink and the mud ceiling had crumbled into the basin, which was now full of dirt.

Camille wasn't sure what to do or say. She would have knocked first, but she hadn't come through a door. So she gave a little cough.

The cats inched in and started hissing at her. This made the woman spin around, wielding the hammer over her head. She spat the nails out of her mouth.

"Who is it?" she sputtered. "D-d-don't think I won't use this!" One of her eyes was blue and wide with fear and the other was shiny and black. This was Ickbee. Though she and Swelda were identical twins, they didn't look completely identical anymore. Swelda's face had become gaunt with age, but Ickbee's was big, pink, and flushed.

"Child of Cragmeal!" the woman said. "Oh my!" She bowed down. "I can't tell you how this makes me feel—so proud, like a wind-caught sail on a tall, tall ship!" She lifted her head and spread her arms wide. "Look at you! My heart's so full it may burst at the seams!" She wrapped her arms around Camille and smothered her for a moment. Camille felt the air being squeezed from her lungs. "Oh," Ickbee cried, "it makes me want to cry to see you after all this time! But that's no good, no good at all." She released Camille, then pulled a handkerchief from her sweater sleeve and wiped her nose. "I've got to get this house propped up before it caves in on itself. And I can't hammer with my one good eye blurred by tears!" She raised the hammer and then quickly lowered it. Ickbee's mind changed gears quickly. "I'm sorry I lost your brother. He's fleet of foot, that one!"

"That's, um . . . okay?" Camille said, though she wasn't so sure that it was.

"This house is tumbling in on itself and it will shrivel if the Ever Breath isn't found," Ickbee said. "The passageway will turn to dust and death! I tell you, death! Both worlds will be lost."

"This is it, then, right?" Camille asked. "The Breath World?"

"But a mere dark corner of it," Ickbee answered.

"But you're one of the keepers of the passageway between the two worlds and"—Camille turned around and pointed to the tunnel—"that's where the Ever Breath once was? In there? In the hand with the broken pinky?"

"Broken pinky!" Ickbee stomped her foot. "It's begun!"

"What's begun?" Camille asked, feeling slightly panicked.

"The hand! If the Ever Breath is gone for too long, the hand will curl up just like that, finger by finger. If it forms a solid fist, the Ever Breath can never be replaced!"

"We still have time," Camille said. "It was only the pinky!"

"It will go quickly now," Ickbee whispered. "Look at them!" She pointed to some wilting roots, the mud around them collapsing onto the floor in small mounds.

"How much time do you think we have?"

"A matter of days. We'll have to find your brother, hope for some communication from your father, and, of course, hope that your father's had luck locating the Ever Breath and—" She broke off and clapped at the mewlers. "Help me here! Start propping this up! I've got to take care of the child of Cragmeal!"

They sulked and hissed, but slowly they moved to the pile of branches on the floor.

Ickbee turned to Camille and said, "But you must be hungry! I forgot. I have food for you. I must seem a dansey-headed fool!" She scanned the counters, the stovetop. "Take a seat! At the table!"

Camille sat down and stared at her brother's glasses. Her eyes were still blurry and she was getting a headache from squinting. She picked up the glasses and impulsively slipped them on. Everything snapped into focus—the mewlers' fur, the roots lining the small hole she'd climbed up from, even the grooves in the table and her own hands.

"Mewlers!" Ickbee cried, clapping hurriedly. "Quick now! Prop, prop, prop! Keep at it!" Ickbee was more in focus for Camille now too. Her face was chubby and round and pretty. Her one blue eye and her one strange black-pearl eye seemed to glitter. She smiled at Camille. "Mewlers are actually quite handy around the house! Good company for an old woman. Bean loaf, bean loaf, bean loaf," Ickbee said, pacing along the counter. "Where is the bean loaf?" She started rattling around under the sink.

The mewlers clattered boards and nails.

"Excuse me," Camille said, over the noise.

"Yes?" Ickbee said. Her head was in the cupboard under the sink and when she lifted it, she struck the back of her head on the wood casing. "Oof!" She rubbed the sore spot. "That will be a nasty welt!"

"I'd like to know what happened."

"Happened?"

"To the Ever Breath," Camille said.

Ickbee collapsed onto the little bed for a moment. "I was robbed! It can happen to anyone. It wasn't all my fault. I'm not the first keeper of the passage to have a problem. I mean, during the flood of 1812, there was that infant sea creature that somehow swam through and took up in some Fixed World sea where I hear he grew quite big and thrived. There have been a couple of blood-betakers, a stray wolven man, for which all of the Breath World is extremely apologetic." She shook her head wearily.

"Do you mean that real magical creatures have gone through that passage from this world to the Fixed World?"

"Occasionally. Just a wee lapse at our end."

"Um, by blood-betakers, do you mean something like vampires? And wolven men, like werewolves? And by sea creature, do you mean, like, the Loch Ness Monster?"

Ickbee chuckled. "I forget all of the strange terms you Breath Worlders have for everything. Loch Ness rings a distant bell—"

"Don't you think you might want to keep a little closer watch on this passageway?" Camille asked, a bit irritated. "I mean, even stores at the mall have rent-a-cops!"

"Rent-a-cops? I'm sorry. I don't understand."

"Fake badge? Stun gun? I mean, you should have this place a little more protected, don't you think?"

"In my defense, since I inherited it, only a very small number of creatures have slipped through. A few urfs who heard rumors of golden pots, a few fairies, one fire-breather— but he was on the small side, about the size of a boar, really, so that's not all that terrible! I mean, I heard that he set fire accidentally to a . . . what do you call them? Mini-mart? In any case, it's nothing compared to the cow-sized fire-breather who did all that damage to your grand city of Chicago! *That* was *not* on my watch! I'll tell you that much."

Camille was stunned. "You might want to look into, um, an alarm system, at the very least!"

"Easy come, easy go . . . but the enchantment was always in place to protect the Ever Breath. Always! This time someone broke the enchantment!" Ickbee spotted the bread basket. "Ah," she said, "I know where I put the bean loaf!" And she jumped up and pulled out a fat roll of something that looked like meat loaf and began to cut it into wedges.

"I brought my lunch," Camille said. She heard a strange buzz. Two fluttering things zipped around Ickbee's head. Ickbee tried to wave them off, but they only flitted over to Camille, who smacked one midair and sent it soaring across the room.

"Small infestation this year," Ickbee said, setting a plate of bean loaf in front of Camille. "Sorry about that!"

"A small infestation of what?"

"Locust fairies," Ickbee said. "They're a tedious nuisance, but nothing more. They keep the mewlers entertained."

"Did I just hit a fairy?" Camille was horrified. Until recently she'd loved fairies! She looked down on the floor and saw a small creature—half fairy, half locust—stand up and dust off her thin wings.

"*Locust* fairy," Ickbee corrected. "A spiteful bunch. My little sister, Milta, always loved these things, carried them around in jars."

"I'm so sorry," Camille whispered to the locust fairy.

The locust fairy eyed her angrily, spat in her direction, and flew up into a cupboard.

"I kind of figured fairies would be nicer," Camille said, hurt.

"Really? Do they have a good reputation in the Fixed World? Here, they're petty creatures, always holding grudges—"

And then the howling rose again—a chorus of loud moaning voices, the same sound Camille had heard in the passageway amid the hammering. "What was that?"

"That howl right there is a blood-betaker," Ickbee said.

Then another, different howl, which was more of a barking yowl, sounded out. Ickbee listened intently and reported, "And that there is the wolven men's cry. Sometimes they sound quite similar when they're riled up or proud of themselves or about to eat someone. Maybe some tea? I should at least offer a child of Cragmeal tea!" She turned a quick, dizzying circle, then put the kettle on to boil.

A brittle, cackling howl rattled the window panes. They both froze.

"And that?" Camille asked. Her stomach tightened into a knot.

"Banshees. Their bark is worse than their bite, except when they're angry. Don't make them angry!"

"I'm not planning on it."

"All of the most vexing creatures know something's wrong. They can sense it, like they do a full moon. They can feel that the Ever Breath is gone." She paused. "Did Swelda give you the gift?"

"The snow globe?"

"Yes. Do you have it?"

Camille unzipped her backpack, pulled the globe out, and set it on the table.

"Shake it."

Camille picked it up and rolled it from one hand to the other. The inner scene was lost in a white swirl, and then slowly the snow settled. There was a mouse in a red vest and a bright plaid scarf, frozen, mid-scamper, in a long marble hallway filled with high-heeled shoes and shiny black leather loafers and pin-striped pant hems. His scarf was sailing behind him, and he had a piece of paper clamped in his teeth.

Camille leaned over the globe. "It's just a little nicely dressed mouse!"

"Ah," Ickbee said. "And so you truly are gramarye, down deep in your bones!"

"What do you mean?"

"Do you think that someone of the Fixed World would be able to look in that globe and see what you see?"

"I don't know why they wouldn't," Camille said.

"Oh, dearie! They'd see a little house strung with Christmas lights or that hefty man in the red suit riding in a sled. You can see what's in that globe because you're of our world."

"Really?"

"Here, we each have our magical gifts."

"Swelda called them magical *afflictions*," Camille told her.

"Is she still talking that way of our world? Oh, how that woman steams me!"

The mewlers had a sturdy branch in place now and were hammering loudly.

"But who's the mouse?" Camille shouted over the noise. "He looks important."

"I don't know," Ickbee said. The howls started sounding out again. They seemed to be echoing from a far-off place, but rolling toward them. "Time will tell. It's the blood-betakers and the wolven men that we have to keep an eye on now."

The kettle let out a shrill whistle that sounded like an alarm. It startled Camille. Her heart felt like a small animal scurrying in her chest.

"How do you think the Ever Breath got stolen?" Camille asked.

Ickbee frowned. "Stop blaming me!"

"I'm not. I—"

"Please change the subject!"

"Okay," Camille said. She had another question ready to ask. "Do you think the blood-betakers and wolven men are riled up or proud of themselves or about to eat someone? Us, for example?"

Ickbee picked up the kettle and poured the hot water into a cup with the tea bag. The tea was purplish and smelled sweet. She set the cup in front of Camille. The steam rose up and warmed Camille's cheeks. It was cold here—cold and damp.

"If the Ever Breath can be returned to its rightful spot in the passageway," Ickbee said, "everything will be fixed. Everything—blood-betakers, wolven men, this house crumbling in on itself. And the worlds won't die. It's simple."

Camille wrapped her hands around the cup.

"How do we get it back?"

"The problem is simple. The solution might be complex. I hope you find the answer to that," Ickbee said, closing the shutters. "You and your missing brother."

"Truman and me?" Camille looked at Ickbee—was she serious? "What about my dad?"

"Ah, well, he requires the telling of a tale. Eat and then I'll speak."

Camille looked at the lump of mysterious bean loaf and thought of her bag lunch in her backpack. Ickbee handed her a fork. Camille wasn't usually squeamish about food, but this didn't look right. Trying to be polite, she speared a piece and put it in her mouth. She didn't recognize a single taste—not one. It was all foreign to her—strange and rich and dark.

"I sent word to your father through Swelda when the Ever Breath was stolen. He and I hatched a plan at this very table. That plan has sent him to very dangerous corners of this world, and I haven't heard from him in weeks. I knew that he would need you two to replace the Ever Breath, one on one side of the passage, one on the other side—the balance of twins. But now I'm thinking he may have hit a snag. He may be relying on you more than we first thought." She lifted her chin. "I have faith in him—and you!"

Camille's next bite was lighter, sweeter, like hitting a sweet swirl in cinnamon bread.

"He made the right decision all those years ago," Ickbee went on. "I know that now. Your father is a forever child. He grew up with his mother and with me, splitting his time between two worlds. I half-raised him, you know. That part of his life has likely been erased." She looked at Camille.

Camille would have liked to tell her that it *hadn't* been erased . . . but it had. In fact, Camille knew almost nothing about his childhood, and certainly no one had ever told her about the existence of another world. The bean loaf now moved from sweetness to a dense sadness—that was the only way Camille could explain it. She tasted grief.

Ickbee nodded and went on. "But then he fell in love with your mother in the Fixed World. He asked me for an enchantment so that he could live a normal life there with her. And although I knew that it meant giving him up, I gave him the enchantment." She shook her head. "It was the right

thing, but it was the hardest thing I've ever done in my life."
Her voice rasped in her throat. "But the enchantment only
works in the Fixed World. When he crawled up from the
passageway three months ago after I sent word to my sister
that the Ever Breath was gone, he was just as I remembered
him. He stood in this room with bits of dirt in his hair and
was my little boy again." Her marble eye glistened in the
lamplight. "And even though he was standing there in front
of me for the first time in ages, I missed him more than ever."

The bean loaf reached a high pitch of taste in Camille's
mouth—and then suddenly it evaporated. The forkful she'd
just put in her mouth melted away to nothingness.

Camille felt a sting of tears in her eyes. She'd never been
able to utter a word about missing her father. She'd buried
herself in disasters and survival stories, but there was something about Ickbee's story, her confession of missing her long-
lost boy, that made Camille whisper, "I miss him too."

It felt good to say it, like handing over a secret that had
started to take on the weight of a rock.

Just then, a mewler leapt onto her lap. Camille stroked its
shiny fur. And though her eyes were filled with tears, she
didn't feel like crying. Then her nose itched, and she
sneezed—three times in a row.

CHAPTER SEVENTEEN

The Death Warning

Edwell's Hops and Chops House was packed. With Praddle perched on one shoulder and the globe hugged to his chest, Truman followed Artwhip, who was being led by the host—a man with bear paws—through the maze of seats. Truman was wide-eyed.

There were horns and hoofs and, on a few well-dressed couples, muzzles. A winged woman talked with great gestures, flapping her wings so hard that the candle on her table blew out. A family with glowing skin beamed in one corner, and a family of foxes, overdressed, sat in another. An elderly woman was eating alone—if you didn't count the arthritic snakes she had for hair curled into a dainty bun atop her head.

One area of the restaurant was reserved for very small tables and chairs, for people who were only knee-high or were in smallish animal forms—raccoon-human hybrids, a few talking beavers. Suspended from the middle of the ceiling by stiff wooden arms was another deck of miniature seating filled with fairies. They were served by a distressed fairy who flew overhead at great speed while balancing a very small tray of dishes covered in metal domes. There were fairies with a variety of wings, some like monarch butterflies, others like dainty moths. No locust fairies, though, that Truman could see.

The food—steaming up from plates and fondue pots, still sizzling on tabletop hibachis, and glistening in the low candle-light—smelled divine. Truman felt a hollow pocket of hunger in his stomach.

Artwhip turned around and whispered, "There he is." He pointed out a jowly, ham-faced man with horns on top of his head—dull horns that looked as if an effort had been made to polish them. "Conveniently forgot to take off his fur scarf. My father likes to show off that he's got money, you see."

The fur scarf was draped around the man's neck. He was talking to the waiter—a lean man about half Artwhip's height, his pointy ears popping up from under his shaggy hair—who was wearing a dark green apron and bow tie.

They could hear Artwhip's father bellowing. "Oh, my son will be here soon! He's just always in a bit of a hazy swodder. You know those dreamy, dunderheaded types. I hope it's no inconvenience!"

Artwhip grunted disgustedly. The waiter turned on his heel and walked away. Artwhip's father now realized he was still wearing his fur scarf. He unwrapped it from his neck, revealing a necktie and a starched collar so tight that it seemed it was choking off oxygen to his brain. He laid the scarf over the back of his chair and then he stroked its fur as if he adored that fur scarf—and maybe he did. *If he loves showing off how rich he is, he probably loves his things*, Truman thought.

When they reached Artwhip's father's table, the sweet

scents of all of the foods had seeped into Truman's head and he felt dizzy with hunger.

"You're late," Artwhip's father said.

"Sorry," Artwhip said. "I lost track of time." He reached out and shook his father's hand with stiff formality. "This is Truman. I'm keeping an eye on him for a friend."

His father's eyes fell on Truman. He cast a suspicious eye over Truman's jacket and shoes made of leaves and his flannel pajama pants, covered with burrs. "Hello, Truman. Is that the latest style? Some kind of beggar chic?"

"Yes," Artwhip answered for him. "It's all the rage."

Artwhip's father looked at Praddle. "Is that a pet? Are pets allowed in here?"

Artwhip ignored the question and pulled up an extra chair from the next table over, which was empty. He and Truman sat down.

"It's nice to meet you, Mr. Ostwiser," Truman said shyly.

"Yes." Artwhip's father didn't look happy. "I'd been hoping to talk to you privately, Artwhip. Father to son, and all . . ." He looked at Truman, who tried to smile politely. "I'll just have to spill the good news, I guess. There's a very plum position opening up in the Office. I could put in a word and end this lowlihood you're wallowing in." He smoothed the slip of hair between his short, dull horns.

Artwhip slouched in his chair. "I was hoping we wouldn't get to this kind of talk until dessert or so," he said, and then he turned to Truman. "Tell my father something about yourself, Truman!" he said, giving a wink.

Right! Distraction, that was why Truman was here. "I'm . . ." Truman had no idea what to say. He couldn't say that he was new to this world and he certainly couldn't say that his father was Cragmeal, King of the Jarkmen. "I'm a fan of Artwhip's hat!"

"Really?" Mr. Ostwiser said.

Artwhip hopped on the new thread of conversation. He pointed to the wooly blue hat on his head and smiled. "It fits perfectly!"

His father looked at the hat and then squinted at Artwhip in confusion. "Fits . . . ?"

"This hat, it arrived today," Artwhip said. "Just in time for the cold weather."

"Why are you talking about a hat?" his father asked.

"Didn't Mother knit this hat?"

"*That* hat?" Mr. Ostwiser laughed as if Artwhip had made a joke. "If your mother wanted to knit a hat, she wouldn't come up with that."

Praddle hissed, and Truman quickly scooped her off of his shoulder and hid her on his lap.

"Take off that ridiculous thing," Artwhip's father said. "It looks like it was knit by an idiot child."

"I'll keep it on, thank you very much," Artwhip said, and it was clear to Truman that these two had a long feud full of little battles.

The elf-sized waiter arrived with two menus. "Should we start with some nibblets?" he asked.

"Can we go ahead and order everything now?" Artwhip said. "I know what I want."

The waiter looked at the menus in-hand, baffled by the change of plan.

"No, no," Mr. Ostwiser said. "Let's look at the menus. No need to cause a rumbusticle!" He chuckled nervously.

"Do you know what you want, Truman?"

"I'd like the sugar-crusted angel bread," Truman said, his mouth watering.

"I know what I want and you always get the same thing," Artwhip said to his father.

"Just look at the menus!" Mr. Ostwiser smiled at the waiter. "Everything has its protocol!"

The waiter coughed. "The customer is always correct. If you want to order without looking at the menus, I can accommodate that."

His father shook his head wearily. He preferred protocol.

"I'll have the baked hen served on a bed of fruit peelings, with clotted-cream onions and steamed blue-veined cheese," Artwhip said. "Oh, and partridge-egg soup. Can we get a basket of lemon-soaked bread heels and the angel bread too? And I'd like fruit water with shaved ice. And the cherry-scented chocolate broth for dessert."

"Is that all, sir?" the waiter asked, but it was obvious that he couldn't imagine there being more.

"Make it *two* cherry-scented chocolate broths," Artwhip said.

"No, no," his father said. "I don't eat sweets."

"They're both for me," Artwhip said. "Trying to put fat on my bones." He patted the dip of his stomach. "Do you want one, Truman?"

Praddle pinched him. "Yes, please," he said.

Artwhip held up three fingers for the waiter.

"And," Truman said, "I'd like something that tastes . . ." He glanced at Praddle.

"Fissshy."

"Is there something fishy?" Truman asked the waiter.

"The pepper-braised milkfish is excellent," the waiter said, twitching his pointy ears.

Praddle pinched again. "Okay," Truman said. "That will work. And I'll have a peanut butter and jelly sandwich," he added.

Everyone stared at him.

"A what?" the waiter asked.

"A peanut butter and jelly sandwich?"

"Who would put peanuts with butter and jelly?" Mr. Ostwiser said, disgusted.

"I can bring you a Danish goosebutter Danish," the waiter offered. "Would that work?"

Truman nodded, embarrassed.

Artwhip's father, his head tilted in a kind of apology, smiled at the waiter and then ordered the mutton, as usual.

The rest of the meal was guardedly polite. They discussed the rolling fog, the possibility of more snow. And as Truman and Artwhip tore into the lemon-soaked bread heels, Mr. Ostwiser asked questions that Artwhip avoided answering. For instance, when his father asked him where he was living, Artwhip told him that he was shuffling between friends. But Truman remembered him saying that he had a landlady, the one who'd spilled chatterbroth tea all over the letter that had come with the hat just that morning. When Mr. Ostwiser asked his son how he was spending his time, Artwhip told him he was looking for a job putting together holiday travel packages. But wasn't he a jarkman? Wasn't he awaiting orders to help the revolution?

Truman tried to distract Mr. Ostwiser. He would interrupt and say "Great bread!" or "Where did you get that watch?" or "Is that scarf made of real fur?" But Artwhip's father was like a steam engine. His questions just kept coming; there was no stopping him. And Artwhip was agitated by the inquisition.

Finally there was a question that put Artwhip over the edge.

"It's time you found someone to settle down with," his father said. "Your mother worries about you. She wants you to find someone who will watch over you. When will that be?"

"I don't need someone keeping watch over me." Artwhip leaned forward. "We have enough hedge-creeps and spies watching over us, don't we?" he whispered.

His father shook his head and answered gruffly, "Don't start. We all need protection!"

"We need spies, eavesdropping on all of us, taking notes on all of us? Do we really?"

His father looked around the room and smiled broadly, as if they were having a lovely conversation, and then he whispered through his gritted, smiling teeth. "You've read in the papers, no doubt, that Cragmeal is Public Enemy Number One and has been spotted with our enemies." Truman wasn't sure how Mr. Ostwiser could speak without moving his mouth.

"Yes," Artwhip said.

"And our good friends the mice signed a contract just last week to keep an extra-watchful eye."

Praddle purred at the word *mice*.

"I read it," Artwhip said in a low voice. "The mice were praised for their patriotism, but they were bought off and they'll now get their protection as they turn people in."

"They could be anywhere." His father picked up a lemon-soaked bread heel and used it to hide his mouth, whispering from behind it. "It's dangerous to even utter things against the Office." His jowls shivered as he spoke, and when his eyes locked onto Artwhip's, Truman saw a taut expression of fear cross the older man's face. "Now that the scoundrel is back, the eyes are everywhere, more than ever."

"He's not a scoundrel," Truman said quietly.

"Be quiet. What do you know?" Mr. Ostwiser said to Truman.

"Don't yell at the boy," Artwhip said. "He's allowed to still believe in heroes."

"Don't say such things!" Mr. Ostwiser reached into the breast pocket of his suit jacket. "I've brought you some of these, Artwhip."

He handed Artwhip a stack of business cards. Half of the face of the card was black and half was white. On the black side, the lettering was white. On the white side, it was black. "Us versus Them!" it read. "The difference is simple!" Artwhip flipped it over. Truman saw an address and the words "Report all suspicious behavior."

"What's this?" Artwhip asked.

"We're widening the net," Mr. Ostwiser said. Truman didn't like the way he used the word *we* to describe what the Office was doing. "Dropping these cards off everywhere we go. You should help the cause. And"—he lowered his voice and slid one of the cards to Truman—"always keep at least one of these on your person, at all times, just in case." He drummed his fat fingers on the tabletop.

In case of what? Truman didn't ask. He was pretty sure he knew what. If he was apprehended in the middle of the night like the man in the tweed suit and blue necktie, he'd have proof that he was Officially Good.

"Take them," Mr. Ostwiser urged.

"No," Artwhip said. "We refuse. Don't we, Truman? We don't need to be reduced to Good or Evil. We are who we are." And he pushed his card across the table back to his father.

Truman followed his new friend's lead. "Sorry." And he slid his card back too.

And that was when the waiter arrived. He was struggling under the weight of a large tray with two plates covered with silver domes. He put the first plate down in front of Mr. Ostwiser. He pulled off the dome and there was the steaming mutton.

"Lovely! Lovely!" Mr. Ostwiser said. "Thank you so much."

As the waiter put Artwhip's plate in front of him, Truman imagined the baked hen, the smell of onions and blue-veined cheese. When was the last time he'd been allowed to eat cheese? His mouth watered. Everything sounded good to him now.

The waiter whipped off the dome, but instead of a hen, there was a broiled rat.

Truman jumped up, knocking Praddle to the floor. Artwhip reared back from the table. His father gasped, covering his mouth with his cloth napkin.

The waiter cried out, "Oh no! I'm so sorry! How . . . ?"

The rat was stiffened in a gnarled pose, its fur singed. Its four claws were sharp and splayed, its tail bent as if broken. It smelled charred and foul. Truman saw a small piece of paper attached by a thin wire to the rat's left hind leg. The waiter moved swiftly and covered the rat again with the dome; then he froze, looking at Artwhip and his father for further instructions. Artwhip was shaking. Truman felt sick. The nearby tables were looking on now, whispering.

"Everything is fine!" the waiter said in a shaky voice. "Please go back to your meals!"

Mr. Ostwiser nodded to the other diners and tried to smile reassuringly.

The waiter tugged on his bow tie, rubbed his pointy ears, and whispered to Artwhip, "Should I take it away, sir?"

Mr. Ostwiser leaned across the table. "What kind of trouble are you in, son?"

"There was a note," Truman said. "Did you see it?"

Artwhip closed his eyes for a second and nodded. "Lift the dome just a bit," he instructed the waiter. "I need to get the piece of paper."

"No," his father hissed. "It could be a death warning. Don't you know that?"

"A death warning?" Truman whispered. Praddle tugged anxiously at his cuffs. He picked her up.

"He's from up in the highlands," Artwhip said. "He doesn't understand anything." He turned to Truman and explained. "In respectable social circles, it's only polite to give a warning if you plan to kill someone—there's protocol for everything." Under his breath he said to the waiter, "Lift it just enough and I'll reach in and untie the note."

The waiter glanced nervously around the room. "It's got an awful feff," he said, pinching his nose. "Move as quick as possible so as not to let out the stench." Artwhip reached in and quickly untwisted the wire, freeing the note. He clutched the note in his fist and put his hand in his lap. The waiter lowered the lid.

Artwhip looked into his father's wet, skittery eyes.

"Well?" Mr. Ostwiser said.

Artwhip read the note in a whisper: "'Artwhip the Jarkman of the Family from Hindman near Toot Hill: Someone is preparing to take your life. You have been fairly warned. Sincerely, T.T.S.'"

Artwhip, his eyes wide, looked at Truman. "So you *are* a futurist," he said.

"Maybe it doesn't have to happen," Truman blurted out. "Maybe we can avoid it!"

Artwhip looked up at the waiter still standing by, and then at his father.

As soon as their eyes met, his father reached into his pocket and placed a wad of bills on the table. He was pale and unsteady as he got to his feet. "Your mother . . . ," he said in a quavering voice. "I won't breathe a word of this. It would destroy her." He coughed as if trying to push down a sob.

Artwhip stood up. "Don't go. Not yet. Let me explain."

"No need. This would only happen to someone who was—" He broke off. "Are you with the underground, the jarkmen?" he whispered. "Is that it?"

Artwhip looked at the ground.

"How could you?" His father's eyes roved around the dining room nervously. "My own son. My Artwhip . . ." And then, incapable of stopping himself, he opened his arms and hugged his son clumsily. Truman thought of his own father and missed him. He felt a tightness of emotion in his chest, his throat.

With his mouth to Artwhip's ear, Mr. Ostwiser whispered, "If this killer doesn't hunt you down, the Office will come after you full of suspicion, ready for capture. The Office knows all. Every jarkman is on their list. Every one. The Office knows things that we can never know! I pray that you can stay alive, that you can keep your soulcase intact. There's nothing I can do for you." With that, he let go of Artwhip and took a few unsteady steps backward. As he tried to find his balance, he grasped the back of his empty chair and his hand fell on the fur scarf. Truman stared as he hurriedly picked it up, wrapped it around his neck, and then walked through the restaurant, grabbing his coat from a row hung on hooks. He gave one backward glance and then pushed open the restaurant door.

CHAPTER EIGHTEEN

The Ruin't Letter

Binderbee Biggby was small—even for a mouse—but he was quick. He'd been posted by the Office of Official Affairs to a nest in the dirt walls of Miss Spottem's cellar for only two days, awaiting some kind of proof of illegal activity from a suspected jarkman, Artwhip Ostwiser. Binderbee had curled his long, thin tail around himself to keep warm, his small, pink ears perked.

And finally it had come, in the form of the nearly ruin't letter.

He'd waited for the jarkman to leave, then tipped over a wastebasket, with a good bit of effort, and collected the letter. He'd folded it up and put it in his briefcase and run as fast as he could to the Office of Official Affairs, nearly getting trampled by some galumphing kid and an angry mewler along the way.

And then he'd slipped along the marbled floors, past all the workers in cubicles and under the humming lights. And talked his way past the secretary into Dobbler's grand gilded office with its mantel adorned with photographs of

Dobbler shaking hands with the most venerable of venerables and his chrome microphone that sent out the alerts and warnings heard from the bullhorn speakers throughout the city. Dobbler even had a private washroom with a lock and key.

And here sat Dobbler himself, the president of the Office of Official Affairs, a strapping man, thickly feathered. Quills peeked out of his suit-jacket sleeves. His nose curved in a hawk's beak. He sat behind the enormous mahogany desk on a leather-upholstered chair with thick golden casters.

Binderbee popped open his briefcase and pulled the letter out. He'd gotten here so quickly that the letter was still damp from the chatterbroth tea, and so he had to be careful. "I've got something good in here! I can feel it! I just need time to look over the evidence, piece it together a little," he boasted, waddling in a frantic half circle to get a better angle on the unfolding of the letter. Binderbee was bowlegged, and this gave him an extra swagger that he tried to live up to.

"We're hoping you mice will pay off," Dobbler said, picking his sharp teeth with a swizzle stick. His desk was covered with blueprints. The sight of them excited Binderbee. The Office of Official Affairs was always looking to expand. On the edge of the desk was a plate with only a smear of gravy and bits of soggy bread left on it. Dobbler smiled at Binderbee. "Do you want to see something?"

"Um, sure," Binderbee said.

"Look at that hat on the peg over there."

Binderbee turned around and saw the hat. It was a shimmering white fedora.

"That's a gift from an old friend of mine from my youth. And watch this!" Dobbler whistled and then lifted his plate and tapped it on the desk. The hat opened in a burst of wings and scattered, then formed a small, quick cloud of locust fairies who swarmed Dobbler's plate, finishing off his gravy and bread bits, in a buzzing whir, until the plate was clean. Dobbler whistled a second time, and the locust fairies shot back to the peg and became a hat again. "Amazing, isn't it?"

Binderbee nodded. "Yes, sir, amazing. But back to this bit of evidence."

Dobbler stood and rolled the blueprints up, tucking them under his arm. He patted Binderbee on the head. Binderbee didn't like that—not one bit—but then Dobbler said, "I have a meeting upland and will be gone for the bulk of the day, but you can use this office. I want you to work until you've gotten all you can from this interception! And remember, Binderbee," he whispered urgently, shaking his meaty fist, the quills quivering, "Us versus Them! The difference is simple!"

This sent a shiver through Binderbee. He loved to be included in the *Us* of *Us versus Them*. Mice had come such a long way—from being on the outside to being in the innermost world. Here. A mouse in Dobbler's office, being treated as almost an equal!

And then Dobbler added in a hushed voice, "I want to take Cragmeal down—no matter what it takes. This evidence had better point in the direction we need it to. Do you understand me? When people get involved with Cragmeal, it's strange how quickly they can become enemies of the Office."

"I don't know what kind of evidence it will be, sir, until—"

"You know what kind of evidence it will be, Binderbee. It will be the kind that helps us nail Cragmeal."

Binderbee stared at Dobbler. Was this how the Office operated? "I can't guarantee that, sir—"

"I'd hate to see a cage with your name on it," Dobbler said with a smile. "You know?"

Binderbee nodded.

Dobbler gave a whistle and the locust fairies flew to him, reforming as a hat on his head. "Darnedest thing, this hat! Amazing!" And then Dobbler strode out of the office.

Binderbee got down to work. *You're a mouse of science,* he told himself. *You work for the Office. You're just doing your job.* He pretended that he'd misunderstood Dobbler. Surely Dobbler didn't want Binderbee to tamper with any evidence, did he? And then Binderbee pretended that the conversation had never happened.

He set the letter up to dry by the fire in Dobbler's fireplace. He jumped on the intercom button and asked the secretary to bring in some supplies—including a tincture known for its ability to seek out original ink marks. He'd studied chemistry at Wesslon University of Technology, where he'd graduated at the top of his class.

By the time the letter was dry, the secretary had delivered the supplies on a silver tray.

"Thank you," Binderbee said, but he didn't even look up, his claws skidding on the shiny surface of Dobbler's desk. The suspected jarkman had told Miss Spottem that she needn't apologize for spilling tea on the letter, that it was likely only from his mother and not very important. Indeed! That was meant to throw any spies off his trail. Binderbee knew better. The letter was important. It *had* to be.

Binderbee picked up the bottle of tincture, squeezed the rubber head of the dropper, and then cautiously let three droplets fall on the page—two small ones and then one big one. He sat back and gazed at his work. The words bloomed on the page.

It looked like this:

your mission.

children are coming

Fixed World.

house of Jckbee in

the Ostley   need a protector. I've

chos   Jarkman. Your heart is

how to stand up

why I'm back again.

worse: the Ever Breath has been stolen.

worlds will per-

ish. I am in pursuit of the Ever Breath

our world, among the most

vicious of creatures. If I

—twins from the long line—to replace the

Ever Breath

trust you will know

down.

I can feel it. I have no time to waste.

Wear this hat. It's how they will know you're one of

us. I've sent word out to the few remaining

jarkmen
of this land. They will help you with this mission.
Sincerely,

King of the Jarkmen

Binderbee said to himself, *Children are coming? Fixed World protector? Ever Breath has been . . . stolen?* He stared at the letter intently until his eyes felt like they were burning. This letter was even more important than he'd thought. He picked up the tincture again. This time he let a droplet fall at the bottom of the page, and there the signature appeared:

Cragmeal, King of the Jarkmen!

He'd intercepted a letter—concerning a mission, no less—from Cragmeal himself! Public Enemy Number One! Maybe this was exactly the evidence needed to put Cragmeal away for good—where he deserved to be!

Binderbee quickly doused the rest of the letter with the tincture until all of it appeared.

Artwhip the Jarkman—

This is your mission.

My children are coming through the passage from the Fixed World. Meet them at the roothouse of Ickbee in the Ostley Wood. They will need a protector. I've chosen you, Artwhip the Jarkman. Your heart is true and pure. You will learn how to stand up for what's right.

You will hear rumors about why I'm back again, but this is the reason and we couldn't dream of something worse: the Ever Breath has been stolen. As you know, if it remains missing, both worlds will perish. I am in pursuit of the Ever Breath. I have been into the darkest parts of our world, among the most vicious of creatures. If I find it, we will need my children—twins from the long line—to replace the Ever Breath in its rightful spot.

Watch over them! I trust you will know how.

I'm writing quickly. Someone is hunting me down.

I can feel it. I have no time to waste.

Wear this hat. It's how they will know you're one of us. I've sent word out to the few remaining jarkmen of this land. They will help you with this mission.

Sincerely,

Cragmeal,
King of the Jarkmen

Binderbee's heart was racing, but he paced slowly around the edges of the letter. He stared at Dobbler's tall bookcase of leather-bound books—books on Office procedures, laws, accounting, the educational parameters of the Academy, and some sanctioned novels and a few collections of patriotic poetry. Then, trying to see with fresh eyes, he glared at the words on the page. The Ever Breath had been stolen. Cragmeal wasn't conspiring with enemies. He'd been trying to find the Ever Breath! Could it be that Cragmeal was good?

As a child, Binderbee would pretend he was surrounded by bad guys—jarkmen, mostly—and had to fight his way out, pretending his tail was a sword. Back then, mice were denied even simple rights. His family, the Elite Biggbys, had to burrow out in the squatters' fields near the shanties. When someone decided to build a home right over theirs, well, so be it. They could move or the diggers would dig them out. There was even a nursery rhyme about it:

> *Mama and Papa going to build a big house.*
> *A house to the sky,*
> *A house without a mouse!*
> *Shoo, shoo, shoo, little measlings!*
> *Diggers a-coming!*
> *Shoo, shoo, shoo, little measlings!*
> *Shoo, little measlings, shoo!*

This nursery rhyme had dogged Binderbee all of his childhood. And now it rang in his head. How many times had his family been out for an evening stroll only to have some child—no matter what kind—come up and start taunting them with it? "Don't listen!" his father had always said. "Chin up! You are Biggbys!" And Binderbee had learned to hold his chin up high and not cry, though he'd always wanted to.

He'd also always wanted to be on the inside, and now here he was. If he tampered with this evidence a little, maybe he'd be promoted. He'd prove to Dobbler he could be trusted. Binderbee clasped his paws, one on top of the other, to stop them from shaking.

Binderbee looked at his reflection in the shiny mahogany of Dobbler's desk. He was a Biggby. He knew what he had to do. He pressed the intercom button and asked the secretary to bring him a cup of chatterbroth tea. It was going to be a long night.

CHAPTER NINETEEN

The Lost Mission

Truman, Praddle, and Artwhip were stalled in the middle of the bustling restaurant, the death warning crumpled in Artwhip's fist.

"What are we going to do now?" Truman asked.

The small waiter with the pointy ears was the one to take charge. He seemed to change in an instant, his features quickly turning steely, his nervous awkwardness gone. He said with authority and urgency, "Let's get you out of here."

Not knowing what else to do, Artwhip nodded at Truman. Truman scooped up Praddle and the snow globe and, together, he and Artwhip trailed the waiter into the kitchen.

The place was steamy and smoky. Chefs shouted over the loud sizzle of meat on long, flat grills, stirred frothy pots, and chopped tuberous roots with fast knives. Waiters came and went, carrying their heavy trays.

Truman looked at the waiters and the chefs. Which one had swapped the baked hen for a broiled rat complete with a death warning? In this confusion it could have been any of them. He hoped that he could find one—just one—wearing a guilty expression. Artwhip was glancing around too. But the kitchen was too fuming, too overrun to be able to tell.

The waiter led them out another door, turned down a hall, and took them through a storage closet filled with boxes of jars and cans. "What are you doing here, anyway?" the waiter asked.

"What do you mean?" Artwhip responded.

"I just don't know why you'd sit there having dinner with your father! That old dough-fart!"

"Hey," Artwhip said. "Watch it!"

Truman stifled a giggle.

"It grates my flesh that you can sit there when there's such an important task to be done. I don't know why he chose you at all. Look at you! You've already gotten a death warning!"

"I haven't been chosen for anything. What are you talking about?" Artwhip asked.

The waiter paused a moment. "Isn't that boy half of it?" he said, pointing at Truman. "Right there."

"Truman?" Artwhip said, arching an eyebrow.

"Half of what?" Truman asked.

The waiter shot Artwhip a dirty look. "Right," he said. "As if you didn't know!" They came out the other side of the storage closet and passed an open meat locker where a woman stood in the cold mist, holding a chain of frozen chickens.

"Good day," the waiter said, in his shy, nervous voice, the one he'd used earlier.

"Hello, there," the woman said gruffly, swinging two frozen chickens by their stiff necks.

Once she was gone from their sight, the waiter looked at Artwhip again and said over his shoulder, "I been in this for five years. You know that? Five years, and not one real thing to show for it!"

"You've been in *what* for five years?" Artwhip asked, impatient. "And where are you taking us, anyway?"

The waiter shook his head, disgusted by Artwhip's stupidity. Finally they arrived at a wide loading door. The waiter opened it to a burst of cold air, and there, down a long alley lined with caged creatures, was a ruckus tent, pulsing with music and noise. "You need to get lost in there," he told them. "Shake off any trail and then get back to your mission. Collect the other half."

"Do you have a mission?" Truman asked Artwhip.

"I don't think so." Artwhip looked at the waiter. "Why should I trust you?"

The waiter smiled and then bent down and lifted his pant leg. There, strapped to his leg by a leather harness, was a dagger just like Artwhip's, with a silver hilt in the shape of the snake with flared plumage on its head. A jarkman's dagger.

"You're a jarkman too?" Truman said.

"Hush," the waiter said, peering around. "I'm Coldwidder."

"I'm Artwhip of Hindman near Toot Hill—"

"I know who you are."

"And I'm Truman."

"I know that too," Coldwidder said, and then he gave a low bow.

Artwhip looked at Coldwidder and then back at Truman. "What's that for?"

"I'd have bowed when I first saw him in the restaurant, but that would have tipped people off," Coldwidder said. "Don't you think?"

"Tipped people off to what?" Artwhip asked.

Truman was pretty sure this had to do with his father—the King of the Jarkmen. He was nervous. Even though Artwhip seemed to be devoted to Truman's father, Truman didn't want to be pegged as the son of Public Enemy Number One. If news got out, he'd have people hunting him too.

Coldwidder considered Artwhip for a moment, as if trying to gauge whether he was kidding or not. "Don't you know that he's the son of Cragmeal?"

Artwhip gasped. He looked at Truman's blue pajamas, the handmade shoes and jacket made of leaves, and the snow globe curled in one arm. "The son of Cragmeal?"

Truman lifted his hand and wiggled his fingers. "Hi."

Artwhip ripped off the blue hat, showing his horns, and bowed.

"You don't have to do that," Truman said. "I'm just a kid. An ordinary kid!"

Artwhip rose. He and Coldwidder smiled at each other.

"Ordinary!" Artwhip said.

"Ha!" Coldwidder said.

"Well, I'm not completely ordinary. I mean, I have medical issues. I have a lot of allergies, and I'm lactose intolerant and I have sports asthma. . . ."

Coldwidder and Artwhip stared at him, baffled.

"I don't follow," Coldwidder said. "What's all that you just said?"

"Never mind." Truman took a deep breath, one that flowed in and out of his lungs, clean and clear. He was used to rattling off a list of his ailments to teachers and camp counselors and coaches, but none of that mattered here. "Let's get back to Artwhip. Does he have a mission or what?"

Coldwidder looked at Artwhip, annoyed by him once again. He threw his hands in the air. "You don't know? What kind of fool are you? You are wearing the hat," he said slowly. "That's how we all can know that it's you. It was in the note." Artwhip wore a blank expression. "You have to know! Didn't you get your note?"

"*What* note?" Artwhip said, and then Truman remembered the story of Artwhip's landlady spilling tea on the letter that had come with the hat.

Artwhip remembered too. "Oh, no," Artwhip said. "It was ruin't. I never read it. Miss Spottem, you see, she only has paws and . . ."

Coldwidder stared at him. "Cragmeal," he whispered. "Your mission is from Cragmeal himself."

"Cragmeal himself?" Artwhip repeated.

"Have you heard from him?" Truman blurted out. "Is he okay?"

Coldwidder looked around in every direction, and low and high too, just in case there were any mice listening in. He motioned for Artwhip and Truman to lean in close.

"You're in charge of Cragmeal's children," he whispered to Artwhip. "You're their guide!"

"But—but—" Artwhip stammered. "Where was I supposed to find them? This one found me! And I don't even know where the other one is—"

"Camille?" Truman said, his pulse racing. "She's not here. She's at our grandmother's house."

"You've got to make it to Ickbee's in the Ostley Wood," Coldwidder said. "Ickbee tends the passageway. You're an Academy boy, aren't you? Rich kids!" He snorted. "They don't teach you the truth in that expensive Academy. Only Office of Official Affairs facts and figures. Their own prissy cleaned-up version of things."

"I know plenty," Artwhip said, indignant.

Coldwidder's face grew serious. "It doesn't matter now. You just have to keep them safe."

"Cragmeal's children . . ." Artwhip was still stunned.

"You got half of your charge right here. You got to find the other fifty percent," Coldwidder said. "And fast."

"I've seen my father in my snow globe," Truman said. "He's all bound up in a museum of strange things. And he's a kid."

"In your snow globe?" Coldwidder asked. "Those things are oldfangled nuisances. You could have been looking at something that happened twenty years ago or twenty years from now."

Truman glanced down uncertainly at the snow globe.

"That's right!" Artwhip said happily. "Maybe I won't get stabbed today! Maybe—"

"He saw you get stabbed in a globe? I'd keep in mind that

the death warning is pretty fresh. It still smells like the broiled rat it was tied to," Coldwidder said.

"But still, are there any museums—dark, spooky ones with chopped-off fingers and dead stuffed creatures?" Truman persisted.

Coldwidder shook his head. "Not that I know of."

"This is what I don't understand," Artwhip said. "Why are Cragmeal's children here now?"

"We're just on winter break," Truman tried to explain. "I think there's been some kind of mistake."

"There's no mistake. You're here for a reason. The Ever Breath," Coldwidder said, glancing between Artwhip and Truman, "is gone."

And then someone back in the restaurant called for Coldwidder. "Where are you? Your customers, Coldwidder!"

Coldwidder clapped Artwhip on the back. "I guess there aren't many free jarkmen to choose from. Almost all of us are in the cages filling these streets or in the bowels of prison. Still," Coldwidder said. "Why *you* and not *me*?" And with that, he turned and shouted back in a shaky voice, "Coming!" The door shut, leaving Artwhip, Truman, and Praddle in the alley.

Down on the alley's far end, the ruckus tent's flaps were snapping in the cold air. Light snow began to float down from the sky. Truman remembered the scene in the snow globe—the blood spreading across Artwhip's shirt, the snowy ground, the tent flaps, the woman in the hood. "Do you believe that the future is the future and there's nothing anyone can do about it?" he asked.

Artwhip looked up at the snowy night sky, the ruffled

moonlit clouds. He said, "The Ever Breath. I've only ever heard people talk about it. It's the breath of A Being Than Which Nothing Greater Can Be Conceived, and it's set in stone. That's what they say. It's set in stone, but that breath . . ." He looked at Truman. "That breath is still alive. It's still breathing. If that's true, anything can happen."

CHAPTER TWENTY

Us Versus Them

By the time Binderbee heard Dobbler's shoes clacking down the tiled hall toward his office, the mouse had written a hasty note with Dobbler's inkhorn and plume. He kept it brief.

Artukip,
Wear this hat!
It's getting cold out!
Keep warm.

Love,
Your mother

And then he'd splashed chatterbroth tea on it until it was illegible and dried it out by the fire. He then, very quickly, put the tincture on it and let the words bleed through.

The original? Neatly folded and hidden in his leather briefcase.

Dobbler strode into the room, wearing his locust-fairy hat. "I'll be here late tonight," Dobbler said over his shoulder to his secretary. "Brew another pot!" Then he spotted Binderbee standing on his desk, next to the fake note from Artwhip's mother. "Ho! Binderbee!" Dobbler said. "You scared me!"

"Sorry, sir. I know mice can be frightful."

"I'm not afraid of mice! Don't be ridiculous. It's just that I forgot you were here." He whistled and the locust fairies darted off his head and onto the peg on the wall. He sat down behind his desk and smoothed some of the rumpled feathers sticking out of his sleeves.

There was a light knock at the door and a man with a jowly face and a tight starched collar poked his head in. He was wearing a long overcoat and a fur scarf. "You sent for me, sir?"

"Oh, Ostwiser. Yes. Come in." Binderbee was startled. Was this Ostwiser a relation of Artwhip Ostwiser the Jarkman? Dobbler went on, "I was just saying I'll never get used to mice working here in the Office. Will you, Ostwiser?"

Ostwiser shook his head. "Doubtful, sir."

This was an insult. *Why wouldn't you get used to us?* Binderbee thought. *We can do just as good a job as you can. Better, if you consider that we can fit into places that you can't! And why sign a contract with us if we didn't deserve to be here?*

"I've called Ostwiser in to hear this firsthand, Binderbee. Sit down, Ostwiser. This is about your son. A serious matter. He's a suspected jarkman."

"My son?" Ostwiser gasped. "Oh, no. Not possible. The boy is on the up-and-up. He's going to apply for the new position in the Confessions Department. He told me so just today." *How cruel,* Binderbee thought, *to bring the father in when he thinks the boy's about to be accused.*

"Really? Well, I hope that's the case," Dobbler said. Then he turned to Binderbee. "Did you find anything in the ruin't letter?"

Binderbee looked at Ostwiser. Would he know that Binderbee was lying if he said it was just a letter about a hat? Would he contradict him and send his own son to jail? Binderbee had no choice at the moment. The fake letter was sitting out on Dobbler's desk. "Sorry, sir," Binderbee said, pursing his lips and wagging his head. "Nothing."

Dobbler looked impatient and tired. His eyes were weighted with fatty pouches for lids. "Nothing at all? Look, I'm working with someone who might know exactly where Cragmeal is and I'm on the brink of getting said person to hand him over to us. And I don't know if you have noticed, but the beasts in the highlands are growing viciously restless. Howling like madmen. The ruckus tents are getting fevered. There are wild fire-breathers starting small fires in the woodlands. There's a restlessness that can't be explained. It's as if the magical creatures are puffing up on their own power . . . as if there's something wrong with the passageway itself, as if the flow of imagination and dream and magic were bogging down somehow . . . as if the Ever Breath itself were gone." Dobbler stared at Ostwiser and Binderbee piercingly. "And my said person might know a thing or two about that as well! If we could get in now, while the power is up for grabs, there's no telling what we could do. And if we can get Cragmeal, once and for all, pegged as the troublemaker he is, if we can make a case to the people of this city that he is a betrayer, that he is the *thief* of the Ever Breath itself, then we can put him behind bars forever. And then we can make a world where everyone is good, and evil is simply done away with."

"But what if he didn't steal the Ever Breath?" Binderbee asked quietly.

"Then we still don't want to miss the opportunity to pin it on him and put him away for good. Evil is evil, Binderbee, and we fight it every way we can!" He drummed his fingers on his desk. "The key to battling evil is to create fear! Then and only then will your people rely on you for protection. Only then will they love you like a strong father. They might not see you as a *kind* father, but they will respect you."

"But—" Binderbee began.

"But what?"

He wanted to say something about using fear and how that was exactly what the beasts did—blood-betakers and wolven men and fire-breathers. He glanced at Ostwiser, who gave the slightest shake of his head, as if to say, *No, don't.* And Binderbee let the air out of his chest. He didn't have the courage. Instead he said, "It was just a letter from his mother, after all, telling him to wear the hat. It's right here if you'd like to read it."

"Why would I want to read a letter from someone's mommy about a hat?" Dobbler said.

"See! I told you so!" Ostwiser said. "My son is a good boy, sir. He truly is!"

And Binderbee felt relieved.

"Fine then, just fine," Dobbler said, but he glared at Binderbee. "Are you sure?"

Binderbee nodded. "I graduated from Wesslon University of Technology, first in my class!"

"A true scholar," Dobbler said, and he let out a mighty sigh. "You two can go, then. I have work to do."

Binderbee started to pack up the fake letter, but Dobbler pinned it under his fist. "Leave this, will you? I think I might need to put someone new on the trail of this Artwhip." Then he glanced at Ostwiser and said through a bright smile, "For your son's own protection, of course."

"I don't think that's necessary," Ostwiser said. His voice jangled with nervousness. "He's very strong and in no trouble!"

"It's just that I've made a deal with this new alliance, as I mentioned." Dobbler looked over at his hat on its peg. "This someone I knew when I was very young, and now has just drifted back into my life. And this new alliance will be a strong one for the Office, especially in the area of surveillance. In fact, even better than you mice," he said to Binderbee.

Binderbee felt heat rise in his cheeks. He wanted to blurt out exactly what he'd learned about Cragmeal to prove that Dobbler was dead wrong about mice. But he held his tongue.

"It's a very kind offer," Ostwiser said, "but you don't need to waste any of your forces on my son. He's just a zwodderhead. You know kids!"

"I'd just hate for there to be a cage with his name on it one day," Dobbler said, in the same slick, threatening voice he'd used when he said the very same thing to Binderbee earlier in the day. "Maybe we can nip in the bud any wrong turns the boy might make. Right, Ostwiser?"

Ostwiser looked down at his hands and nodded. "Yes, sir."

Dobbler turned to Binderbee and held out his palm. Binderbee climbed onto it. This was the most embarrassing part, relying on Dobbler's hand for a ride down off the desk. Dobbler set him on the floor.

Ostwiser was holding the door open, and as Binderbee marched out of the office, Ostwiser was saying, "Anything else you need, just call me, sir! I'm at your disposal."

"Shut the door on your way out!"

Ostwiser and Binderbee walked past the secretary's polished hooves and down the long marble hall. Ostwiser was jotting a note of some kind. Just before he headed into the maze of cubicles and Binderbee headed toward the building's lobby, he said, "Binderbee."

"Yes?" Binderbee said.

Ostwiser bent down and stuck out his hand for Binderbee to shake. "You didn't have to."

"What? I don't understand."

"I'm saying thank you," Ostwiser said.

"I don't know what you're talking about," Binderbee said, but still he shook Ostwiser's hand.

Ostwiser handed him one of the black-and-white business cards. "Us versus Them," Ostwiser said, but his tone wasn't the rah-rah chipper tone that Dobbler had used. Ostwiser's tone was serious. He looked Binderbee in the eye, and then, strangely enough, the fur scarf around his neck writhed and a set of eyes appeared, giving a wink.

Binderbee gasped.

"The card," Ostwiser said. "Take a look at it when you get a chance. Brand-new design."

"I will," Binderbee said.

"Promise?"

Binderbee laughed. He thought Ostwiser was joking around. But Ostwiser didn't laugh.

"Okay," Binderbee said, suddenly serious. "I promise. I'll take a look at it."

"Tell my son," Ostwiser whispered.

"Tell him what?"

"You'll know what to tell him." Ostwiser gave a nod and walked on down the marble hall back toward the offices.

Binderbee watched him go, then scratched his head. Once he walked out through the revolving door into the cold, whipping wind, he looked at the card. It was plain, black-and-white, similar to others he'd seen before. And then he flipped it over.

There was Ostwiser's scrawl:

Save my son. You'll need help. Go to Otwell Prim. Ogre Herdsman of Fire-Breathers. Jarkman. Old friend of mine. back before I worked for the Office. Be quick and true of heart.

Ostwiser, with his fur scarf and jowls, was going to buck the Office? He was going to help Binderbee? Could Ostwiser be a secret agent? Who was Us and who was Them?

Binderbee wasn't sure anymore. But he could use the help and protection of an ogre.

Binderbee folded the card in half and then into quarters, stuffed it in his briefcase, and ran through the revolving door into the cold foggy air.

CHAPTER TWENTY-ONE

Into the Ruckus Tent

To get to the ruckus tent's open flaps, Artwhip, Truman, and Praddle had to walk down the alley, passing by a row of caged creatures. Truman didn't want to look any of them in the eye. The man in the tweed suit had spooked him. And so Truman tucked in his chin as if simply trying to keep his neck warm. He decided to distract himself by asking questions.

"Why do they have ruckus tents?" he asked Artwhip. "What are they?"

"They're sanctioned by the Office of Official Affairs only in that the Office doesn't care much what goes on inside of them. The Office's stance seems to be that if folks go in there and become so unruly that they injure themselves, well, so be it! There has to be an outlet for madness of various sorts, and the Office has decided that this is the place. A container for chaos."

The alley was narrow and they were passing by the cages so closely that they could hear the creatures breathing. Some were moaning. Truman saw the sad eyes of a two-headed fox, pacing a circle in its cage under one of the US VERSUS THEM! posters. Truman looked away quickly.

"Do you know anyone with the initials T.T.S.?"

"I've been running through everyone I know," Artwhip answered, "from my Academy days, my old neighborhood, my new neighborhood. . . . I can't think of anyone."

"Why did the note writer use initials, anyway?"

"In death warnings, only initials are required," Artwhip said, "which always seems a little cowardly to me. If you're going to kill someone and you're giving due warning, shouldn't you at least sign your full name?"

"It seems unfair that you'd have to spend your time trying to figure out initials instead of getting ready for the person who's coming to kill you," Truman said.

"Exactly," Artwhip said.

They were at the tent flaps now, about to go inside, but then they heard a screech echo down the alley. A vulture had one of the cages gripped in his claws. Beating his broad wings, he lifted the cage up into the night sky.

"I saw a whole flock of vultures last night," Truman said. "They were all carrying cages."

"Things aren't right," Artwhip said. "C'mon." He grabbed Truman by the shoulder and they hustled into the tent.

The ruckus tent had a lofty top, propped up by poles. There were actors and actresses in cake makeup and thick, velvety costumes reciting lines while clomping across wooden stages raised above the dirt floor—not to mention jugglers. When Truman and Artwhip stepped into the tent, there was a woman—just about a foot tall—spinning overhead, hanging on to a cloth swing by her teeth.

But the ruckus tents were also loud and foul-smelling and overpacked. There were bullhorn speakers in here as well, but Truman could barely hear the warnings above all the noise. One hand on the hilt of the dagger hidden under his coat and shirt, Artwhip led the way, past a row of drunkard booths selling Clamberskull, onion ale, vino delight. Praddle sat on Truman's shoulder and named all the strange creatures. Keg-bellied horned men and urfs, even a few glowskins (who glowed more brightly when drunk), were chanting and singing and falling all around the dirt floor. Passing by a small group of knurls, he heard one whisper, "Down with Cragmeal! Traitor!" Bleary-eyed, they lifted their drinks.

A drunken fairy, flapping just a few feet off the ground, flew right into Artwhip. She crashed to the ground, crumpling one wing. "Curse you!" she said. "Curse you!" And then she began to cry.

"Too late," Artwhip said. "Already cursed."

The beggars swarmed anyone who walked into the tent. Some had sealed eyes and others had nubbed wings. They cried to Artwhip and Truman, "Just a bit for me and me babes at home. They're stomach-sick, sire. Just a bit . . ."

"Hold on to what's yours," Artwhip said to Truman over his shoulder.

Truman tightened his grip on the snow globe and Praddle, and kept marching forward as fast as he could.

"Come, come, sire, you've got a soft heart, no?"

"Spare just a coin? Just one coin for a beetle-eyed beggar!"

"You have to say no," Artwhip said. "It's hard, but you have to."

"I don't have any money," Truman said. "Sorry, I really don't." He was caught in a small crowd for a moment, and when he looked up, he saw Artwhip talking to a woman wearing a long cloak. A hood was blocking her face from view, but Truman was afraid that he would recognize her face. She might be the woman he'd seen in the globe, that very first scene where Truman had seen Artwhip bleeding in the snow.

"Excuse me," Truman said to the beggars. "Sorry, I don't have anything. Excuse me." He fought his way to Artwhip's side and grabbed his shirt. "Sorry to interrupt. I have to tell you something."

"Just a second," Artwhip said, not even looking at him. His eyes were fixed on the woman. Over the hooded cloak, she also wore a shawl. She was young and willowy thin, with skin the rich color of mud. And although her skin was dry, almost as if covered with scales, she was beautiful. Her eyes were shiny and golden, like honey. "This woman is telling me something important."

"I was just saying that someone stole my money pouch, and I'm supposed to bring medicine back to the bog for one of our newborn bog-colts. And now I've gotten turned around and I'm so hungry that I'm light-headed."

Artwhip looked a little lovestruck and seemed tongue-tied. "Um, uh, sure," he said. "Here." And he gave her all the money in his pocket.

"Thank you," she said, and then she stuck out her hand. "I'm Erswat."

Artwhip shook her hand. "Artwhip."

Truman coughed, as urgently as he could. "Artwhip! I need to talk to you. Privately."

The woman looked at him and smiled, waiting for an introduction.

"Oh," Artwhip said. "And this is Truman—and his mewler, Praddle."

"Nice to meet you." She didn't seem like a killer, but Truman was still suspicious. Nothing here was quite what it seemed to be. And hadn't he seen her there, at the scene of the crime? "This place prinkles my flesh with fear," she said. "But we're supposed to love it, aren't we."

"I think we are," Artwhip said. "But I don't like it either. It's just too much."

The bogwoman looked at him, surprised that they had this in common.

"I think I'm going to throw up," Truman said. "I have a lot of allergies and a strong gag reflex."

"Are you ill?" the woman asked.

"Very!" Truman said, shoving Artwhip away from her. "We have to go! Nice to meet you."

"Hey," Artwhip said, "stop shoving!"

"Well, thank you again. I won't forget this," she said to Artwhip. "I hope you feel better," she told Truman. And she gave a nod and then blended into the crowd.

Artwhip stood there, frozen in place, and watched her go.

"She was the one!" Truman said.

"What one?" Artwhip asked dreamily.

"The one who was there in the scene when you were stabbed. *She* might be your killer."

"I don't think so." He smiled and gave a laugh.

"But that was her! I swear!"

"That beautiful bogwoman? I think I'd let her stab me if she wanted to."

"If you're dead, you can't fulfill your mission!"

"I know, I know," Artwhip said.

They turned down one aisle between stalls and then another, in hopes of losing anyone on their trail. They passed a bookseller with a magnifying glass, plucking small bookscorpions out of the innermost pages of an encyclopedia. A horn sharpener was filing the horns of a young horned man to sharp points.

A bear wearing a blue tuxedo was refusing to ride a bicycle for his trainer. They were arguing back and forth.

"I need more money than this! Who can work under these conditions for so little pay?"

"You signed a contract!"

Finally the bear roared, but then politely took off his top hat and jacket, handed them to the trainer, and strode away.

Then they saw a sign that read GLOZELIA THE FAMED FUTURIST. The stall was swathed in gauzy purple silks and Glozelia wore a glittering robe and veil. She was studying the skittering paths of mice in a pen. She closed her eyes, flung back her head, and with her arms outstretched, she shouted, "Ruin! Ruin!" And then she hissed, "Unless . . ."

No one was listening except Artwhip and Truman, who paused for a moment. "Unless what?" Artwhip asked.

The futurist snapped her focus onto Artwhip. She lifted her veil and, parting her long, shiny black hair, revealed a second mouth on the back of her head, "You! It's you, is it?"

"You're a turn-mouth!" Artwhip cried.

Truman had never heard of such a thing—someone with two mouths.

"It *is* you!" she said sharply.

Artwhip looked around. "I guess it is me."

"You are but a breath-body." Her second mouth moved quickly, the words tripping from her lips. "Your soulcase is in grave danger. Be careful! Death watches!"

Artwhip froze. He looked stricken with fear.

"It's okay," Truman said. "Come on. Just keep going. She probably says that to everyone!"

Truman pushed Artwhip on and they started walking more quickly, turning down aisles at random. They made so many turns that Truman no longer knew which direction they'd come from.

"Haven't we shaken everyone on our trail by now?" Truman asked.

"Yes, but . . ."

"Are we lost?"

"Not exactly. It's just that I don't quite know where we are."

"That's called being lost."

"Hmm . . . ," Artwhip said.

He turned around abruptly and there, at his side, was an old man holding an aged accordion.

"Which way is out?" Artwhip asked. "Do you know?"

"I was going there myself," the man said. "I need a bit of help. I'll show you the way if you'll each take one of my arms and help me out. I have a carriage waiting."

Artwhip looked at Truman, who shrugged. Truman was keeping an eye out for the bogwoman in her hooded cloak.

"That's a deal," Artwhip said. He hooked one of the old man's arms and Truman hooked the other. They helped steady him.

"Turn left at the end of this aisle," the old man said. "Have you had a lovely time tonight?"

"Lovely isn't the way I'd describe it," Truman said.

"I don't like these places," Artwhip said.

"There's a lot of madness tonight. What with"—he lowered his voice—"the new charges thrown at Cragmeal. Public Enemy Number One."

Artwhip didn't say a word. Truman knew that he wasn't supposed to talk about Cragmeal.

"Some of the people might feel safer if he's caught," the old man said. "But there are many, many who would feel lost and beaten without a king, even if he has been gone so many years."

"I guess you're right," Artwhip said, trying to sound neutral on the matter.

They walked past a stand where someone was selling brine-boiled nuts that smelled so good that Truman's mouth watered. His hunger must have shown, because the old man stopped. "May I buy you two bags of nuts?" he asked. "As payment for seeing me safely out of the ruckus."

"No, no, that's not necessary," Artwhip said.

"I'm allergic to nuts," Truman said, but it was more of a habit than something he actually believed true. He hadn't sneezed or coughed or wheezed or swelled up or felt itchy or nauseous since he'd arrived here.

"I insist," the old man said. "I had a very good night. I'm quite a good music maker, you know. Lots of patrons." He pulled out a purse of coins and ordered two bags so quickly that they didn't have time to protest. Not that Truman would have. He wanted the nuts.

The music maker handed each of them a bag—warm and already a little oily.

They walked a bit farther down an aisle and, finally, there were the tent flaps. Truman's knees trembled. He knew what might be coming.

They stepped out into the wintry air. The street was just as he remembered it from the snow globe. It was quiet and empty. Snow covered the ground, and it was still coming down. And there was the straggly dog in the cage, but now that Truman was in the scene he could tell that it wasn't a dog. It was a wolf.

"I've got it from here," the music maker said, and he pointed to a carriage, parked just a bit farther down the road. Truman looked over his shoulder, keeping an eye out for the woman in the hooded cloak. "Before you go," the music maker said, "I have to tell you that you remind me of my lost son." He gazed at Artwhip.

"Oh," Artwhip said.

"He labored to breathe from birth, but he'd be about your age, had he lived."

"I'm so sorry," Artwhip said.

Truman felt bad for the old man, but he was nervous. "We have to get out of here," he whispered to Artwhip.

"Do you mind if, well, this is a strange thing to ask, but I'd like to put my arm around you as a father would a son," the music maker said. "To see just how tall my boy would have been, just what his shoulder would have felt like under my broad arm."

Truman tugged on Artwhip's shirt.

"Well," Artwhip said, holding the bag of warm, oily nuts to his chest. "I'm kind of in a rush—"

"Ah, well, don't worry then," the old man said. His eyes filled with tears. "You have a busy life. I know that."

"No, no," Artwhip said, sucking in a breath. "It's fine. But, you know, just for a moment."

And so the music maker smiled and reached up and put his broad arm around Artwhip's shoulders. For just a split second Truman remembered the hug Artwhip's father had given Artwhip in the restaurant, a strong embrace, so sad too. And then Truman thought of his own father—what it was like to be hugged by him at the end of a long day. He suddenly remembered exactly what his father's aftershave smelled like, even when it was masked by the fried-food Taco Grill smell. And, for a second, he forgot about this strange world and the Ever Breath. All he remembered was being at home—with his mom and his dad and Camille.

And then he looked back at the tent and saw the woman in the hooded cloak, and he grabbed Artwhip and yanked his arm as hard as he could. Artwhip staggered backward and cried, "Ow! What was that?"

And the music maker lifted his hand, revealing a small dagger. "Sorry," he said. "Had no choice in it! If you don't die, I'll be in terrible trouble."

Artwhip pulled his own dagger from under his shirt, but it slipped from his hand onto the snow. "You're T.T.S.?"

"No! Just the hired assassin!" His dagger trembling, the man took a few steps toward Artwhip. "You're going to die, right?"

Praddle sprang, her teeth bared, and bit the man's leg. He swung his leg around and kicked her off. She landed hard in the gutter.

Truman scrambled forward and grabbed Artwhip's dagger. He stood in the street, pointing it at the man. "Don't take another step!" he shouted.

"I had to do it!" the music maker cried. "The Ever Breath is hanging in the balance! Please die!" And then he gave a sad finger-wiggling wave, and Truman noticed that the wave had something wrong with it. The music maker was missing a finger—his pointer was gone. Not even a little stub remained. Truman's mind flashed on the museum he'd seen his father bound up in, and the missing finger wearing a strange ring preserved in a glass case. The nine-fingered music maker turned quickly and started running down the street. He was light on his feet, not that old at all.

Artwhip lay in the snow not far from the caged wolf, who was growling. Truman scrambled to his side.

"Nicely done," Artwhip said. "You scared him off."

"I don't think I'd have known what to do if he'd come at *me*." Truman held the dagger out to Artwhip.

"You hold it for me for now," Artwhip whispered. A snowflake landed on his cheek and melted. "He'd have done me in for certain, but you were here. Thank you." Artwhip's shirt was already spotted with blood. Truman's hands were shaking. He wasn't sure what to do. Praddle sat by Artwhip's shoulder and meowed.

"You're really bleeding," Truman said.

"Just a small wound," Artwhip said, but he looked pale and frightened.

All at once the woman in the hooded cloak was at Artwhip's side. She was breathless. "Get a flesh tailor. Quick!" she said to Truman.

"A flesh tailor?" Truman said, deciding the woman was not the threat he'd thought she was.

"Erswat." Artwhip said softly. "You came back."

She lifted his shirt. "You need a flesh tailor. It's serious." She took off her shawl, and as she used it to stanch the blood, Truman saw webbing, thin and fine, between her delicate pink fingers. "What happened to him?" she asked Truman.

"He was stabbed by this man with an accordion," Truman said. "A hired assassin!"

"I don't need to be stitched up! I'm fine," Artwhip insisted, but when he lifted his head he looked dizzy.

"Maybe we need Coldwidder," Truman said. "Maybe he'd know what to do."

Artwhip shook his head. "Not him!"

The wolf growled in his cage. "Back when I was a jarkman," the wolf said, "we didn't get stabbed in the streets and lose our daggers. In the old days we battled at Bull's Noon or got charred by fire beasts. But never this foolishness."

"He really doesn't need to hear that now," Truman said.

Artwhip winced. "It's true. I got stabbed by a plain old music maker and I'd even had a death warning. I'm worthless!" He let out a moan.

"Go get Coldwidder," Truman said to Praddle. "I want to stay here with him."

"Go fast, mewler!" Erswat said.

Artwhip shook his head, but he didn't have the strength to fight it. Praddle took off like a shot.

Erswat was taking a tincture out of her pocket. Using a dropper, she dotted the wound with a blue liquid. "This will speed his healing," she explained.

Three locust fairies buzzed around over their heads amid the snowflakes. Artwhip sighed. "More locust fairies."

"Go away! Shoo!" Erswat said.

Truman waved his hands in the air and they zipped up overhead and hovered.

"I have to go," Erswat said. She then began to cough so loudly it seemed to rattle her whole body. "I have to make my way back to water. But if he needs me, call to me."

"Call to you?" Truman asked. "How?"

"Why, through the water, of course," she said, laughing a little, as if Truman had been joking. "Just call to me!"

"Oh. Of course!" Truman said.

The bogwoman put her hand on Artwhip's forehead and started coughing again. Despite her apparent suffering, she seemed to want to stay longer. "Keep your eyes open," she said. "You must be quiet and still." She wiped the damp hair from Artwhip's eyes and pointed up at the sky. "Snow blossoms," she said. "Just look at all the blustered snow blossoms coming down!"

And then she stood up, curtsied to the two of them, and headed down the street.

Truman took Artwhip's hand and looked up at the night sky. "It's going to be okay," he said, hoping it was true. But even as he said it, he heard his voice quaver.

A group of loud men wearing kilts over furred legs came barreling out of the tent, singing, "Oh, but I love her, Rosamund Rose! Oh, but I love her today!" They swayed like drunken bulls. "Tomorrow's not clear! But with a song in me ear, I love Rosamund Rose today!" They slid around in the slick snow, and, arm in arm, kept each other up until one went down and the others followed. The largest of them landed next to the snow globe, which in the confusion had been left on the snowy street. He picked it up and shook it. "Whose is this?" the man shouted.

"Over here!" Truman said.

The man popped up and skidded over on his wobbly legs. "Oh, my Rosamund Rose!" he sang, handing Truman the globe. "Tomorrow's not clear! But with a song in my ear . . ." He linked arms again with his buddies and they wobbled on down the road.

Truman held up the globe. There was Ickbee's hut surrounded by trees, and there, among the trees, were dim lurching beasts—baboonish, short, and muscular, with broad hunched backs and wide lower jaws, long snouts, and close-set eyes. Fangs, yes—they had long white fangs.

And there was a figure looking out the window, just as there had been the last time he'd seen Ickbee's hut in the globe. But this time the window looked crooked, as if being weighed down by the hut, which seemed to be on the verge of collapse. Through the crooked window, he saw a face. This time it was not an old woman with mewlers on her shoulders.

It was Camille, wearing a blue woolen hat and clutching a hammer to her chest. And for some strange reason, he heard her voice in his ear—a soft but insistent whisper. *Truman, where are you? Where have you gone?*

But how could he hear her? She was stuck in a globe—in the past, the present, the future? Truman didn't know for certain, but still he whispered back, "I'll be there. I promise."

And Camille's face in the snow globe looked startled. She glanced around and then up at the sky as if she'd actually heard him and was looking for the source of his voice.

"I know where my sister is," Truman whispered to Artwhip. "I know where we have to go from here."

"Erswat's shawl," Artwhip said dreamily. "She forgot her shawl."

CHAPTER TWENTY-TWO

Otwell the Ogre

Binderbee had made his way over hoof divot and wagon rut and through tall grasses, and was now skirting the bog. The snow was deep for him and the trip was slower going than he'd expected, but still he hurried as fast as he could. The wind, strong and sharp, came in whirling gusts. It cut through his vest and chilled his bones, and every once in a while it whipped up so fast that Binderbee was afraid an air current would lift him right off his feet.

What would his father think of him now? Out in the weather, Binderbee Biggby of the Elite Biggbys on a quest for the Ever Breath itself. He imagined his father telling him it was an uppity quest for a mouse, even a Biggby, but smiling just the same, proud of him. His father had been dead for some years now. He had died in a wheezy makeshift house on the weedy edges of town. His soulcase had given out, letting his soul loose in the world. *His soul could be with me right now*, Binderbee thought. *Right now!* This was a comfort.

He stopped to catch his breath, gazing at the bog. He could see the writhing paths of sea serpents, and downstream, on the far bank, a bog-horse was nuzzling her two small dragonlike bog-colts, with their scaly skin and wobbly legs.

He could see, too, the mud-slick homes of the bogmen that lined the far shore. Half in the water, half out, the homes looked as if they were settling into a stew of peat and silt. Near one of the houses, he saw a shape moving in the distant fog, and then another. They were bogmen, rising from the brown water, lifting their silt-silken arms and pulling themselves up on land. There were three of them, slick and shining black and wet, soaked to the very bone. Two had fish that they placed in a bushel basket on the shore. Then Binderbee heard a woman start to sing—a bogwoman—and he knew he should clap his hands over his ears. But it was so beautiful, he couldn't.

> Oh, body, do not give up this night.
> Body, turn, rise up, turn!
> Oh, body, do not give up this night.
> Body, rise up, rise up, turn.
> Oh, body, burn on your driving light.
> Burn on, thy body, yes, burn.
> Oh, body, burn on your driving light.
> Burn on, thy body, yes, burn.

Binderbee stood in that spot, unable to move, unable to turn away from the song. He thought of his mother piling blankets on his father as he was dying, trying to keep him alive, warm, how she rubbed his feet with her paws and kept his lips wet with water from a rag. It was the most beautiful song he'd ever heard, and he was lucky that the bogwoman stopped singing, because only then could he remember that he was supposed to be looking for the Ever Breath, only then could he remember that he was trying to make it to Otwell's house in the Webbly Wood, only then could he return to himself.

He shook the song from his ears, combed his whiskers, and wondered if he'd have frozen to death in that spot if the song had gone on, for that was the legend of the bogpeople. He didn't want to think about it.

He pressed on through the reeds on the soupy edges of the bog, and at length he smelled a wood fire. He climbed onto a rock and, with a broader view, saw a trail of smoke in the sky—what might well be a sign of Otwell Prim's chimney at work. He clambered down and strode along quickly now. And soon enough he saw the mailbox with "The Prims" written on it in white letters.

A long path led to the house. As Binderbee headed down it, he saw an ogre with a squarish head and large nostrils. The ogre had a swollen eye, so puffed it was almost sealed shut. He was staggering around his yard, holding a broken broom handle. His wife, who'd sunk to her knees, was crying in the yard. She was a banshee and her cry, sharp and keen, hurt Binderbee's sensitive ears. It was a rude change from the bog-woman's song, that was for certain.

The smoke that Binderbee had seen wasn't coming from a chimney, however. It was coming from the charred remains of the house itself. It sat hollow and blackened—all that was left was its stone foundation.

Off to one side was a broken fence, and beside it, a smoldering barn. A few domesticated fire-breathers were sniffing the smoky wind and nibbling at the burnt tufts of grass that showed through the snow.

Binderbee peeked out from behind a tree. The ogre looked confused and terribly sad. Was he crying too? Binderbee was sure he saw tears. How tough could a blubbering ogre be? Binderbee screwed up his courage and walked toward the ogre.

"What has happened here?" he asked.

Frightened, the ogre brandished his broken broom handle. "Who's there?"

"Me!" Binderbee shrieked as loudly as he could. "Down here!"

"Oh," the ogre said, "a mouse."

Binderbee didn't like the way he'd said that. *Oh, a mouse.* It was offensive. But Binderbee was used to this kind of insult. He rolled his eyes and proceeded. "Who was here?"

"Three wild fire-breathers," the ogre said. "They tried to take over my herd."

"They burnt us to nothin'!" the banshee screamed furiously. "Devils! Every one of them!"

"I've been sent to you for protection," Binderbee said. "Ostwiser sent me. Aren't you a jarkman?"

The ogre looked at his wife.

Her eyes were fixed on the mouse.

"No one's called me a jarkman in a long time," the ogre said. "But I am and always will be a jarkman and proud of it." He raised himself to his full height.

"Cragmeal's children are coming through," Binderbee whispered. "They're set to arrive at the home of Ickbee in the Ostley Wood. The Ever Breath is gone."

Otwell stared at him, steely eyed. He paced back and forth amid the rubble.

"What's all this?" the banshee cried. "What are you two plotting?"

"You've come to the right ogre," Otwell said. "I'll do whatever I can to help!"

"The air's still warm from the breath of those beasts," the banshee said, "and you're going to leave me!"

The ogre ignored his wife. "Let me go get my best weapons." He marched into the burnt house.

His wife followed, shouting. "Leaving me with all of this mess to clean up, are you?"

He emerged a few moments later with a blackened sword, a dagger, and a switchblade fitted into scabbards strung around his meaty middle.

The banshee was yelling at him still. "You haven't touched those things in ages! You're all wobbly in the waist now! You'll be beat in two seconds! All of your swordsman medals have tarnished, you know!"

He whistled for his fire-breather and it trotted up from where it had been grazing. It had a massive scaled body, a smoking snout, and restless spiny wings that were obviously too small to lift its body into the sky. "Settle, Chickie," he said, petting the fire-breather's long neck.

His wife was still berating him. "Mark my words, you'll get yourself killed and then you'll have me to answer to! I'll say 'I told you so! I told you so!' for the rest of your miserable life!"

The ogre bent down and put out his hand for Binderbee to jump onto. "Woman," he said gruffly to his wife, "this is a jarkman mission. Jarkmen protect and serve. This is my duty, regardless of whether I myself live or die!"

The banshee sighed. "I didn't even get a slab of meat for your swelped eye!" she said.

"I'll be fine."

"Did you actually win medals?" Binderbee asked.

"When I was a boy in the Academy. That was long ago and far away," Otwell said.

"Does the fire-breather fly?"

"Nope. These domesticated ones fatten up and can't quite muster the wing strength." And then he looked at Binderbee. "Would you like to sit in my breast pocket? That way you'll have a view."

"Yes," Binderbee said, tightening his grip on the briefcase containing Cragmeal's letter. "Thank you!"

And so it was that Otwell Prim the Ogre of the Webbly Wood and Binderbee Biggby of the Elite Biggbys set off for Ickbee's roothouse in the Ostley Wood.

CHAPTER TWENTY-THREE

Battle of the Blood-Betakers

It was growing dark now and Truman could barely see the path. Coldwidder was up ahead. He'd stolen a delivery wagon from Edwell's Hops and Chops House and Artwhip was in the wagon, mumbling in a restless sleep. Coldwidder was pulling, Truman was pushing. Praddle was keeping Artwhip's chest warm, lying across him like a small fur blanket, and the snow globe was wedged in near Artwhip's back.

The snow was sifting down through the trees, which seemed to be closing in. The forest was filled with howls and moans. Now and then, low rooting grunts would come from the bushes.

"They know something's wrong," Coldwidder said. "They can sense the passage's weakness. Even if they don't understand it, their magical energy isn't releasing into the Fixed World. The flow is diminished. They're becoming wilder, more full of themselves, more living-dream."

Truman thought about this for a moment. He remembered what Swelda had told them about the Breath World and the Fixed World, how they depended on each other.

"Does that mean that my world, the Fixed World, isn't getting enough of things like magic and imagination and dreams?" Truman asked.

"It goes both ways! That's the *point* of a passageway," Coldwidder said angrily.

"You don't have to get mad at me," Truman said.

And then the front wheel hit a rock, shooting Coldwidder forward onto the ground. Coldwidder jumped up and brushed himself off roughly. "You do understand that both worlds could die, right?"

Truman nodded.

"I'm allowed to be a little testy! Cragmeal could have picked *me* for this plum position of guide and protector. But no. I'm called in to clean up the mess!"

"Look," Truman said, "it's my father who's missing, and my *actual* guide who's been stabbed, and my very own sister who I last saw being surrounded by strange monkeylike creatures with fangs! I get that this is a difficult situation! Okay?"

"Okay," Coldwidder said apologetically. He grabbed the handle. "Heave-ho! Keep pushing!"

As Truman and Coldwidder made their way over the rough terrain, the howling grew louder. Truman was cold and shivering. His back was sore from being bent almost in two, pushing the wagon, and his legs felt like rubber. Worst of all, the howls seemed to have burrowed into his bones. Each one vibrated within him, rattling his ribs.

Eventually Coldwidder lifted his hand. They came to a stop. Artwhip mumbled something about mutton in his sleep.

"The hut is just up a ways, around this curve," Coldwidder

announced. They stood there silently for a moment, listening. The snow was ticking on the earth around them, but then there was another howl—a call that echoed through the woods and was met by a responding howl and then a third.

"They're circling," Coldwidder whispered.

"What *are* they?"

"Blood-betakers," Coldwidder said.

Then there was the snap of a tree limb not far off. Truman looked in the direction of the sound. He thought he saw something glitter in the trees—small and low to the ground—but then, in an instant, it disappeared in the snow-dusted underbrush.

"We're not alone," Coldwidder said. "Let's hurry."

They moved as quickly as they could, bumping the wagon over ruts and roots. At last Truman could see a flicker of light through the windows of Ickbee's hut, which was puckered and crumbling. In fact, this was exactly the way he'd seen it in the snow globe: there was Camille in the window, wearing the blue hat, the hammer gripped to her chest.

"It's Camille!" Truman said, but then he realized that the shadows would be shifting, just as they had been in the globe. He looked out among the trees and there he saw three forms lurching in the darkness, moving among the trees. "Hurry up!" Truman urged.

"Going as fast as we can!"

"Slow down! Watch the snow globe!" Truman was worried about it crashing into the side of the wagon and smashing to pieces.

"Fast or slow? Which is it?"

A blood-betaker roared.

"Fast!" Truman shouted.

Coldwidder and Truman were running toward the door, the wagon with Artwhip in it jostling between them. The blood-betakers saw them and let out a chorus of yowls as they started to run through the trees. Truman could hear their feet pounding on the ground, getting louder and closer. Artwhip, lying in the wagon, was being jostled and banged along.

"Hey," he said hoarsely. "Where are we?"

Praddle nuzzled under Artwhip's chin, hiding her eyes.

The door to Ickbee's hut swung open just as they arrived.

"Oh my! Yes! The boy is back! Let them in and shut it quick!" Ickbee cried.

Coldwidder ran in, giving the wagon one last hard yank to get it inside. Truman flew in after him, knocking into a few mewlers along the way. Camille rushed to slam the door, but there in the gap was an arm—furred and muscled—and its clenched fist. Camille threw her weight against the door and so did Coldwidder and Truman, but the arm was attached to a fiercely strong blood-betaker, who, with one shove, sent the three of them sprawling across the floor.

The door banged against the wall, dislodging the fragile dirt ceiling so that parts of it landed on the floor in large chunks. The beast roared in the doorway.

The mewlers arched their backs and hissed.

Truman saw that Camille looked awful—puffy-eyed, red-nosed. "Are you okay?" he asked.

"Been better," she said. "Interesting outfit."

"You're wearing my glasses!" Truman said.

"How did we get here?" Artwhip said, looking dazed.

"Don't move!" Truman shouted.

Praddle pawed at Artwhip's shirt, trying to keep him down. Some other mewlers jumped up on Artwhip to help her. Artwhip was too weak to fight them.

The blood-betaker roared again, and then licked his fangs. A few locust fairies darted around the room, disappearing into cupboards, wedging themselves under quilts.

"The woodstove!" Coldwidder said. "Use it to set something on fire. Blood-betakers are afraid of fire."

"The house is falling to pieces!" Ickbee shouted. "The woodstove is dead!"

Truman saw that the stovepipe was completely disconnected from the wall. They'd have to fight. He pulled out Artwhip's dagger.

Camille looked at him, her eyes wide. "Do you know how to use that thing?"

"No," he said. "But I can try."

Coldwidder pulled his dagger out of the harness on his leg and lunged at the beast. The blood-betaker only smiled, took a few heavy steps into the kitchen, and swiped at him with his claw. Coldwidder dodged and the blood-betaker landed on the kitchen table, smashing it to rubble.

Ickbee screamed and waved her rolling pin over her head.

Camille was on her feet too, wielding the hammer.

Now another blood-betaker was at the door and the third was pushing his way in from behind and letting the door swing shut. The second one threw his weight into the room and grabbed Truman by his jacket. He pulled him in so close that Truman could feel the beast's hot breath in his face.

Camille struck the blood-betaker in the leg with the claw of the hammer. He roared and, still holding Truman in one arm, grabbed the back of her jacket.

Praddle sprang at the blood-betaker, digging her teeth into his arm, but it barely fazed him. He snapped at her with his massive jaws and then swung her off. She hit a wall and slid to the floor, limp.

"Praddle!" Truman shouted, but she didn't move.

The other mewlers, their tails curled between their legs, backed away from the beasts.

The blood-betaker who had crushed the table had Coldwidder cornered, and the third blood-betaker was eyeing Artwhip in his wagon—as if he were a tasty dish on a plate. Ickbee struck the beast on the back of his skull with her rolling pin. He looked at her in brief confusion and then reached out, grabbed her, and held her in a headlock.

They were all pinned or cornered or in some way defeated.

This is it, Truman thought. *The end. They're going to devour us. We're going to die here. Painfully.*

"This may be an awkward time to say it," Ickbee said to Truman, "but I am awfully sorry I almost cracked your head with a rolling pin."

"That's okay," Truman said. "No harm done!"

Everything was silent for a chilly moment except for the low, happy growls of the blood-betakers.

And then, by some strange miracle, the front door was thrown open again and there stood a massive man with a squarish head and one swollen black eye. "Sorry to interrupt! Otwell Prim here, Jarkman Ogre from the Webbly Wood, with my fire-breather Chickie!" He let out an angry war whoop and brandished a huge, gilded—if slightly charred—sword.

The angry, well-armed ogre named Otwell Prim had a mouse in his breast pocket—a well-dressed mouse wearing a clever little smirk. The mouse gave a hearty wave. "Binderbee Biggby here!" he shouted, and then he let out a war-whooping squeak.

Praddle lifted her head and blinked.

"Praddle," Truman whispered, relief flooding through him. "You're okay."

She gave a small nod.

They were backlit suddenly by a hot flare of fire that shone through the windows in a bright flash. The fire terrified the blood-betakers. They let go of Ickbee, Camille, and Truman and shuffled to the corners of the hut, where they cowered, snorting fearfully.

"Settle down now, Chickie," Otwell the Ogre said over his shoulder. "I think we can handle this peaceably. They're just some frightened blood-betakers, after all!"

CHAPTER TWENTY-FOUR

The Enchanted Letter

Binderbee, the little mouse, was pacing circles on the wood floor. He was flushed with excitement and couldn't stop saying, "I've never come to someone's rescue before! I mean, not like that! It was really something, wasn't it?" The mewlers eyed him hungrily, but kept a polite distance.

Everyone else in the room was still a little stunned.

Otwell Prim had ushered the blood-betakers out of Ickbee's crumbling hut at swordpoint. And with a few encouraging bursts of flame from Chickie, the blood-betakers darted off into the woods. Otwell strode back into the room. "Well, now! Off to get the Ever Breath, aren't we?"

The room was quiet.

Then Camille said, "Excuse me, but who are you two?"

"Otwell Prim, Herdsman of Fire-Breathers—"

"We know that!" Coldwidder broke in. "Why are you two here?"

Binderbee picked up his briefcase and popped it open. "I uncovered a letter from Cragmeal!" he said, and he pulled out the original tea-stained letter and gave it a shake.

"A letter from our dad?" Truman said.

"Ah, so you are, in fact, the children of Cragmeal!" Binderbee said.

Truman and Camille exchanged a glance, then nodded.

"Imagine that!" Otwell said with a smile, and then he gave a deep bow. "At your service!"

"Thanks," Camille said.

"No need to bow," Truman added.

"Are you sure the letter is from our father?" Camille, always a little suspicious, asked. She pushed Truman's glasses up the bridge of her nose.

"One man's trash is another man's treasure," Binderbee said.

"Hey," Artwhip said, sitting up in the wagon. "That's the letter that came with my hat. You stole that from me! That's my mission!"

"No, no, no. You threw it away. I *saved* it!" Binderbee said.

"Can I at least read it?" Artwhip asked.

Binderbee handed it to him.

"We'd like to read that after you're finished," Camille said with some agitated impatience in her voice.

"I was head of my class at Wesslon and was a very good scientist," Binderbee informed them. "I used a chemical to draw out the original deposits of ink. I read that letter and knew that Cragmeal was for the good, and I wanted to do all I could to help him find the Ever Breath and help clear his name." He turned to Artwhip. "And then your father seemed to know that I was trying to protect you and Cragmeal, and he sent me to find Otwell Prim—to help me on this quest."

Artwhip looked up from the letter, confused. "My father? Helped you protect me . . . and Cragmeal?" He laughed. "My father is Official Affairs through and through. He'd never do that."

Otwell spoke up then. "But he did. Your father, once upon a time, was a jarkman himself. But then when you were born—"

"A jarkman?" Artwhip looked paler.

"Well, he worried that being a jarkman would make his life too dangerous. He joined the other side—for your sake."

Artwhip stared at the letter in his shaking hands.

"Love can make you do things you never thought you'd do," Ickbee said.

"Can we see the letter now?" Truman asked.

"Do you mind?" Camille added.

Artwhip handed it to them.

Truman and Camille sat down on the small bed and spread the letter on their knees. It was a full page, scribbled in their father's handwriting, but the words looked pale, and as they tried to read the letter, some of the words faded and others darkened.

"It's disappearing," Truman said.

"What do you mean?" Binderbee asked.

"The words," Camille said. "Not all of them are staying on the page."

Ickbee walked over. "Read the words that you see," she said. "It could be an enchanted letter. Your father could have prepared for the chance that you would see this letter with your very own eyes. An enchanted letter allows for the right message to reach the right people."

The page looked watery, almost translucent. And soon there were only seven words left:

I

will

stand

dream

Watch over   *you*

Truman felt a great rush of love. It swelled in his chest. He looked at Camille. She was teary-eyed. Her chin quivered once and she bit her lip.

"What does it say?" Artwhip asked.

"It's part of a song, that's all," Camille said. "One that he sang to us every night."

"But it means he's really here," Truman added. "I was waiting for some kind of proof. This is it!"

Camille reached into her jacket pocket and pulled out the photograph that Swelda had given her. "He's a forever child here. Swelda gave me this."

Truman cupped the picture in his hands. "It's him. The boy in the museum—I saw him in the snow globe!"

"What museum?" Camille asked.

"One with all kinds of strange exhibits and dead animals and a chopped-off finger in a glass jar," Truman said excitedly. "He's really here and he needs us!"

Camille shook her head. "Don't get all emotional. We have to keep thinking logically about everything or we'll turn to mush!"

"Camille," Truman said, his voice quiet, "things are different here. Can't you feel it? This place, in some strange way, belongs to us—or we belong to it."

"Yes, yes, heard it before. We're gramaryes. We're magical—we'll have our magical afflictions or our magical gifts. Right. Fine. But—"

"I heard you talking to me," Truman said. "I was looking at you through the globe and I heard you and I talked back to you and you heard me too. Didn't you?"

Everyone's eyes turned to Camille.

"Did you hear him talking to you?" Ickbee asked.

Camille looked at the letter in her hands. "Yes, I heard him. I didn't want to really believe it. Just that one time, though."

"Ha-HA!" Ickbee exclaimed. "And did you hear him with both of your ears?"

Camille thought about it. "Just my right ear," she said.

"And I only heard you in my left ear," Truman said.

Ickbee clapped. "Just like Swelda and me and our seeing eyes! Ho my! Ho dear! See how the long line lives on?"

"They're really gramaryes," Otwell said.

Artwhip and Coldwidder were smiling. Binderbee nodded and shook his small fist victoriously.

"Let's not make a big deal about it," Camille said. "So we

can hear each other speaking—where we come from, people do it all the time with cell phones."

"I think it *is* a big deal," Truman said. "A very big one."

Camille handed the letter to Artwhip. "Here. This really belongs to you."

"No," he said. "You keep it."

Camille looked at Truman. "Do you want it?"

"Yes," he said. "But I don't have any pockets."

Truman could tell that Camille didn't want to hold the letter. Something about it scared her. Maybe she was afraid because it did mean something to her. As she folded the letter gently and slipped it into her pocket with the photograph, Truman saw that her hands were shaking, ever so slightly.

●　●　●　●

Over the course of the next half hour, everyone moved quickly. Ickbee held up what looked like a fisherman's tackle box. "My stitchery kit! I'll stitch up the bleeder. I'm not a flesh tailor, exactly, but I do know how to sew."

"Are you sure it's necessary?" Artwhip asked.

She inspected the wound, nodding away. Coldwidder helped move Artwhip from the wagon to the couch. Ickbee handed him Truman's snow globe. "Gaze upon this," she said. "Take your mind off the pain." Artwhip held the globe but squeezed his eyes shut, and she set to work.

Meanwhile, Coldwidder and Otwell helped load things onto Chickie's scaly back. Ickbee had canteens for water, a lantern hooked to a pole, and a fire-starter kit, which, with a fire-breather on the tip, seemed a little silly to Truman and

Camille. But they did as they were told and prepared food, with instructions from Ickbee to unload her cupboards into deep rucksacks—root jerky, hardened fatty lard cakes, tins of stew, fresh tarty-tarts. Truman handed out woolen clothes knit by mewlers—lopsided hats, sweaters with different-length sleeves, three-fingered gloves. Truman, Camille, Artwhip, and Coldwidder bundled up in layers of clothes—Otwell was too large and Binderbee too small for any of the items.

Finally Ickbee finished her row of tidy little knots on Artwhip's chest, and Chickie was loaded up. Except for Otwell, who was outside making sure that Chickie had enough bark to eat, everyone was huddled around Artwhip.

"You okay?" Coldwidder asked Artwhip. "If you ride on Chickie and the rest of us walk, you think you can make the trip?"

Artwhip nodded. He pushed himself up and swung his feet to the floor, wincing through the pain of his stitches. "Truman, Camille, how about you tell us what you see in the globe one more time before you go?"

Truman and Camille rushed over, shook the globe, and stared into it. It was empty except for the snow itself—a white slate—and then words emerged:

To find the Ever Breath and your evil father
Meet me in the Dark Heart.
                    T.T.S.

"Who in the world is T.T.S.?" Artwhip shouted.
"What's the Dark Heart?" Camille asked.

"I'm not sure I want to know," Truman said, seething over the word *evil*.

"Camille," Ickbee cried, "look in *your* seeing globe!"

Camille had hidden her globe in a cupboard and now she whipped the door open and pulled it out. "It's the carved wooden hand on the Ever Breath's pedestal!" She shook her head and then turned to look at the others, her face slack and pale.

"And?" Truman asked. "What's wrong?"

"The hand," she said. "It's about halfway there."

"Halfway where?" Artwhip asked.

"It's almost closed up," she said. "Into a fist."

Otwell came back into the hut. He barely fit, what with his hulking shoulders and the walls caving in. He noticed the quiet intensity, the faces shadowed with gloom. "What's wrong now?"

"We're headed into the Dark Heart," Coldwidder said.

CHAPTER TWENTY-FIVE

Snow-Rooting Fire-Breathers

"You'll have to travel straight through the night. There's no time for sleep," Ickbee said.

"We should arrive by dawn." Coldwidder paced back and forth. "If we don't get attacked too many times."

Truman didn't like the sound of that, but he didn't want to ask any questions just then. They had to hurry.

Ickbee was staying behind, defending her post. "I can't leave my mewlers and the passageway. Someone's got to keep propping up the hut!" she said as the mewlers climbed over and around her with nervous energy.

Artwhip, Coldwidder, Otwell, and Binderbee—in Otwell's breast pocket—said their quick farewells to Ickbee.

But when Truman and Camille came up to say goodbye, Ickbee grabbed them, hugged them to her chest, and began to cry. "I know that you have to go, but I hate to see it," she told them. "Be careful! Promise me?"

They promised, their voices muffled by her sweater.

Then she released them, but she kept on crying and

blowing her nose into her hanky. Once they'd left, she waved the hanky at them from the doorway of the withering hut.

Praddle was poking along through the snow, hopping from fire-breather footprint to fire-breather footprint, following Coldwidder up the path.

"Praddle!" Truman called.

She turned around.

"You should stay here," he said.

Praddle shook her head and mewled defiantly.

He ran to her and picked her up. "Come on," he said, rubbing her between her ears. "Ickbee might need you."

She stared at him and then purred, "Be carrreful!" She jumped from his arms and ran back to the house.

"Aren't you allergic to those creatures?" Camille asked, sniffling.

"Nope! Crazy thing, huh? I always wanted a dog. Why not a mewler?"

"Hurry up!" Coldwidder shouted. He was up front leading the way—already a hundred yards uphill—holding the lantern on the long pole to help light the path. Camille and Truman got in line behind the fire-breather, with Artwhip on her back, and Otwell and Binderbee.

Truman wasn't sure what to think of the expedition. They were closer now. They had a destination. He was with Camille again. All of these things felt right, but he was full of dread. Plus, he was already freezing cold. It was dark outside now and the wind was whipping up. It had felt wonderful to exchange his leafy jacket for a knit one, along with mittens and hat and extra socks, but the mewlers were lousy knitters and all of their stitches were wobbly, with gaps and holes and snags. The wind needled through.

He caught up to Camille and was about to ask her if she had any ideas, but she started talking before he had a chance.

"Remember when you were going through the passageway, there was the small room with the pedestal of the hand?" she asked.

"Yes," Truman said.

"I found husks in there."

"Husks?"

"Dried exoskeletons of locusts," she said. "Now I wonder if locust fairies shed their exoskeletons like locusts do—when they're ready to fly."

Truman remembered stepping on something in that room, something with a strange fragile crunch. "Do you think they crawled in somehow and then, once they could fly—"

"They airlifted the Ever Breath out!"

Truman and Camille ran ahead up the path.

"Listen!" Truman shouted. "Camille's figured something out!"

"What if the Ever Breath was airlifted out of the passageway by locust fairies—"

Binderbee hushed them. Everyone stopped and looked at him. "I forgot to mention that we might be tailed by someone from the Office of Official Affairs," the mouse whispered.

"Perfect!" Coldwidder said.

"I hear those types stab first and ask questions later," Otwell said.

"They're not our only problem," Coldwidder said. "We smell like a hops and chops house with all of Ickbee's food on us. We're a walking feast. We'll lure all kinds of beasts to us, smelling like this."

"If locust fairies stole the E.B.," Binderbee whispered, "who put them up to it? They couldn't have been acting alone." Sitting in Otwell's pocket, he reminded Truman of a hood ornament on a very large car. "You know," he added, "Dobbler has a hat—one that he's very proud of—a fedora, actually, made of living locust fairies."

"I once saw a robe of locust fairies," Truman said. "Only the hem of it. I was hiding in a log. I never saw the person, though I do know that the person was very small and was wearing little boots."

"I don't care what my enemy's fashion tastes are! I want to know who we're about to face in the Dark Heart," Coldwidder said, trying to keep his voice down.

"Me too," Otwell whispered. "A band of warlocks? Wild fire-breathers?"

Chickie let out a plume of angry flame. Domesticated fire-breathers didn't like wild fire-breathers.

"We've got to be prepared for all of them," Coldwidder said, "at any time. Especially as they'll smell us coming."

"What can we do?" Truman said. "We need the food!"

"I refuse to part with food," Artwhip said. "I have a rule against that."

"Me too," Otwell said in his low, sonorous voice.

"Personally, I'm not that hungry," Camille said. "I ate bean loaf and it didn't really agree with me." She belched. "Excuse me."

"And I have a rule against getting popped in someone's mouth as a side dish!" Binderbee said.

"I'm pretty sure that the colder it gets, the more calories we burn just trying to keep warm, much less climbing up a mountain," Camille said.

"Calories?" Coldwidder asked. "What are they?"

"Never heard of them," Artwhip said.

"Do you think there's a museum in the Dark Heart?" Truman said.

"Ha!" Coldwidder said. "No! Of course not!"

"How many times have you all been there?" Camille asked. There was an uncomfortable silence.

"Well?" Truman prompted.

"Um, I've never been," Coldwidder said

Camille turned to Otwell. "Maybe you've been there?" He shook his head.

"Binderbee?" Truman said.

"No," Binderbee replied.

Artwhip raised his hand. "Never."

"You see," Coldwidder said, "not many people have actually survived a journey into the Dark Heart."

"Are you serious?" Truman asked.

"Look at it this way," Binderbee said. "If we don't go and try to help, we'll all die anyway!"

"Oh, that makes me feel a lot better," Camille said.

A quiet intensity settled over them. It was dark now. They kept hiking in the moonlight through the snow-blanketed fields, with the wide-open, starry, wind-whipped sky overhead. Truman saw a herd of golden-horned rhinoceroses nestled around a protective outcropping of rock.

"Winged night-serpents," Artwhip said, pointing up. A flock of strange long birds glided by.

"Do you feel like you're being watched?" Truman asked Camille.

"Stab first, ask questions later," she answered under her breath.

Slowly but surely, the snow was getting deeper and the paths steeper as they headed up the mountain.

"I once read about surviving in the Alps in winter," Camille said. "I think we're supposed to take long strides, heels first. It's the best way to cover ground quickly in the snow."

They all tried it, but still it was hard work, especially for Coldwidder and the kids, who had such short legs. Truman was the smallest kid in his class, after all. And how much strength did he have left? His legs were sore, and the shoes Praddle had made for him, now stuffed with wool socks, were raising blisters on his heels. Plus, it was bitter cold.

"Wait," Artwhip said. "Are you sure this is the right way?"

"Are you questioning my ability to set a course?" Coldwidder barked.

"Are we lost or aren't we?" Binderbee said.

Camille leaned over to inspect one of the ogre's footprints. "This snow doesn't look good," she said.

"Snow is snow!" Coldwidder said.

"It's layered," she said. "Packed snow is a good sign. Layered snow is a bad sign."

"A bad sign for what?" Truman asked.

"Avalanches, actually," Camille said. She had taken Truman's glasses off and was wiping them on her sleeve. "Do you have those here?"

"Avalanches!" Coldwidder gave a snort. "This isn't

avalanche country. We only have avalanches out near where the snow-rooting fire-breathers live, out in banshee territory."

"Does anyone else see that?" Artwhip asked, pointing across the snow.

"See what?" Otwell said.

"The smoke," Artwhip whispered.

Truman looked out across the snowy field, lit up by the fat, bright moon, and saw tendrils of smoke spiraling up from the snow—ten or fifteen spirals. "Where's the smoke coming from?"

"Snow-rooting fire-breathers," Artwhip replied.

"That's impossible!" Coldwidder said. "We're clearly far from banshee territory and so there can't be any snow-rooting fire-breathers, as they have been semidomesticated by banshees."

"Except that there *are* snow-rooting fire-breathers!" Binderbee shouted. "Let's get out of here, Otwell!"

The ogre took one thunderous leap, and there was a cracking sound, a rumble.

"Don't run! You'll only shake things up!" Camille shouted.

Everyone stopped and stood still except Coldwidder. He was looking up at the sky. "Isn't that the North Star?" he asked.

"What do fire-breathers do?" Truman whispered.

"They tend to attack and then *roast* people," Artwhip whispered back.

"Now, now, let's not be so dramatic about it," Coldwidder chided. "Sometimes they only singe you."

"If I get singed because you got us lost—" Binderbee began.

"The banshees can call fire-breathers off," Otwell said. "I'm married to a banshee. I'm actually almost fluent in Banshee—from listening to my mother-in-law bad-mouth me for years."

"Listen," Camille said. "Just in case there is an avalanche, you should try to get to the edges of it, where the snow is finer. And swim. I've read about it in books."

"Swim? In snow?" Coldwidder said. "That's idiot-speak right there!"

"I'm serious," Camille said. "All of the books tell you to make these swimming motions, very quickly, while the snow is still light and on the move. If it hardens, which happens fast, you'll get stuck and you can suffocate and die. And if you get stuck, try to punch your hand or kick your leg out above the surface so that someone can dig you out."

"The fire-breathers dig tunnels, which makes avalanches more likely," Artwhip said.

"Did you learn that at your precious Academy?" Coldwidder scoffed.

"I did," Artwhip said. "And I learned that once they smell food, snow-rooting fire-breathers send grunting calls through the tunnels and start to swarm."

"Does this look like snow-rooting fire-breathers to you now, Coldwidder?" Binderbee said. "Hmm?"

The others looked around and saw that they were standing in the middle of a loose ring of smoke plumes.

Coldwidder was flustered. He started stammering, "W-w-w-we've got to . . ."

"Keep calm," Artwhip said. "Maybe they only want our food."

Just then, a fire-breather's head popped up from the snow. Truman thought it looked like a terrier's, at first, with shaggy fur and soft brown puppy eyes, but then he noticed the ridge of spikes that started at the back of its head. Chickie let out a whinnying snort of flame. This was one of her relations, but it was obvious she was afraid of it.

When the fire-breather turned its head, grunting out some kind of call to the other fire-breathers, Truman saw the boarlike tusks. And then other heads popped up, one after the other. The fire-breathers bared their teeth, and with each grunty breath, smoke spun up into the air. They heaved themselves to the surface and, pawing the snow with their long, thick claws, they tightened the circle. Truman stared into the face of the nearest beast. He saw a small blue flame flashing behind its teeth.

Otwell put his hand on the hilt of his sword, but as soon as he did, the fire-breathers started growling in fiery gusts. He let go of the weapon and raised both hands in the air. "Peace!" he said. "We're here in peace!"

"I'm going to open a rucksack and feed them," Artwhip said.

"You're crazy," Coldwidder said. "That will only put them into a frenzy. We've got to run for it."

"No," Camille said, "we can't."

"If we all run on the count of three—" Coldwidder said.

"No," Camille said, "all of our footsteps will start an avalanche."

"Banshees!" Otwell said. "Hear them in the distance?"

Truman heard a high, warbling, grief-stricken call.

"They're signaling our deaths!" Binderbee said. "I'm with Coldwidder."

"One," Coldwidder said.

"No," Camille said.

"Two," Coldwidder said.

"Let's just try feeding them," Artwhip pleaded.

"Three!" Coldwidder said, and with that he sprang forward and leapt over the nearest fire-breather.

Truman and the others ran too. Bolting in different directions, they confused the fire-breathers, who ran after them, shocking bursts of flame shooting from between their blackened teeth. The banshees' cries sounded louder, closer, but they were soon drowned out by the rumbling that started up again in full force. The sound rose until it was deafening. Snow was charging down the mountain toward them.

Truman shouted for Camille, but she couldn't hear him. She was soon swallowed by whiteness. Truman was too, but he remembered what Camille had told him and he started to swim. He kicked his feet and swung his arms over his head. He swam as hard as he could, trying to keep his head high. He felt battered and overwhelmed, but still he kept swimming.

And once the rumbling ended and the snow stopped falling, he began to dig upward. He dug until he saw light and finally he was breathing the cold, windy air.

There was Camille up ahead of him, Truman's glasses sitting on her face cockeyed, and Artwhip was there too, next to Chickie, who was shaking snow from her scales. They were both panting.

Truman wiped the wet snow from his face and looked downhill across the snowy field—nothing but white stretching down and down.

"Where's Coldwidder?" Artwhip asked.

"And Otwell and Binderbee?" Camille added.

"How could we lose an entire ogre?" Truman said.

Just then there was a distant trembling, and a massive boot kicked its way up through the snow.

"Otwell!" Artwhip exclaimed.

Artwhip, Camille, and Truman ran to him, their legs puncturing the deep snow. They dug as quickly as they could.

"I've got an arm!" Camille shouted.

"So his head might be over here," Truman said, digging fiercely until his hand touched something rubbery—the ogre's nose. Otwell's face gasped to the surface of the snow. His beard was iced.

"Binderbee?" he said, muscling his way to a sitting position.

Binderbee, still holding on to his briefcase, crawled out from his pocket. "Present and accounted for!"

"But what about Coldwidder?" Artwhip said. "Coldwidder, where are you?"

"Hopefully he tried to punch his way out. That'll give him a pocket of air," Camille said. "But we don't have much time."

"We need help," Otwell said. "We need to call in the banshees."

"What can they do?" Binderbee asked.

"They can call the fire-breathers to order and the fire-breathers can sniff and dig him out," Otwell said.

"And then turn him into a piece of toast?" Binderbee said.

"It's our only chance," Camille said.

The ogre whistled a tune that was sad and mournful. The banshees started keening in the distance.

"Let me do the talking," he said, and he whistled again.

The banshees rushed in, ghostlike women with wild hair floating around their scowling faces. Their crying voices were high-pitched.

Truman clapped his hands over his ears.

"They sound like dolphins!" Camille said.

"Really depressed dolphins!" Truman added.

The banshees whirred around their heads.

Otwell raised his voice as high as an ogre's voice could go. "We've a pimso, yah, but wee high." He stuck out his hand to indicate Coldwidder's height. "And he's been eldbit by the windary and white knoffs. Could you bit-bit the fire-brays to brindle through the knoffs and loft him upwith?"

The banshees cried and wailed and gnashed their teeth. One whirred forward and shook her head, and her hair waved as if underwater. She responded rapidly and sharply to Otwell's request.

Otwell held up one finger and bowed, and then turned to the others to translate. "We have to give her all of our food in payment."

"That's preposterous! We'll starve out here!" Binderbee protested.

"We don't have time," Camille said. "We have to give it to her."

"Or else," Truman said, "the firebrays will loft the wee pimso upwith but they'll take their time and he'll be dead!"

Camille stared at him sharply. "Did you just speak half-Banshee?"

Truman shrugged.

"We'll give them everything," Camille said, pulling the rucksacks off Chickie's back. "Come on!"

Artwhip and Truman pitched in, untying the sacks and throwing them toward the banshees.

"We are frissling our nosebags," Otwell said. "Haste-please, will you criigle and toot the firebrays?"

Banshees swooped down and grabbed the sacks as they appeared and dashed off, spiraling into the air and then to the distant trees, except for one. She opened her arms and cried out, "Criiiiiigle! Criiiiigle!"

Truman could hear the fire-breathers tunneling toward them through the snow. They popped their heads up like prairie dogs and gazed adoringly at the banshee. She screeched her command and the fire-breathers set off, wildly bursting and snorting through the snow. They moved quickly, forcefully. And it wasn't long before one rose up and let out its smoky grunts and the others came barreling over to help. In no time they'd unearthed Coldwidder, lantern pole and all, and nudged him out of the deep snow with their spiky heads and tusked snouts.

"Get away from me! Don't touch me!" Coldwidder was screaming, swinging the snuffed-out lantern on its long pole.

"He's a little blue around the gills," Artwhip said, "but he's still Coldwidder. Alive and well."

The banshee whirred up, her hair spinning like a fan, but

then she descended again. She cried out something that sounded like a warning.

Otwell squinted at her, confused. "A brottle that's swipping from every prindle?"

"What does that mean?" Camille asked.

"She's warning us that we're being swipped from every prindle!" Otwell said, looking into the dark shadows of the surrounding woods.

"Stop speaking Banshee!" Coldwidder cried.

"We're being watched at every turn," Otwell said.

"Ask her who's watching us," Artwhip said. He had taken the lantern off the pole and was using the fire-starter kit to relight the wick.

"Whoowhit?" Otwell asked.

"Dezzles yev fleet blinkers," she screeched as she flitted up and off. The snow-rooting fire-breathers followed, tunneling through the snow, trailing their puffs of billowy smoke.

"What did she say?" Camille asked.

Otwell kept scanning the woods. "*Dezzles* means millions and *fleet blinkers* are quick eyes."

"Do you think Dobbler has sent an army?" Artwhip asked.

"An unseen army?" Coldwidder said, his eyes darting from side to side.

"It doesn't matter," Artwhip said, climbing onto Chickie's back. "We have to push on. We've lost time and we're off course. We need to pick up the pace."

They all agreed.

"I think I know a shortcut that'll put us closer to the Dark Heart." Artwhip, still holding the pole lantern, climbed onto Chickie's back. "If you don't mind, Coldwidder."

"Fine," Coldwidder said. "It was the stars that were off. They can be tricky."

They quickly fell into line and started marching single file into the forest.

"How about you send back some tarty-tarts from the rucksack," Coldwidder said to Artwhip.

"Um, about that . . . ," Binderbee said.

"What?" Coldwidder said.

"We gave all our food away—in exchange for your life," Artwhip explained.

"You did what?" Coldwidder said, looking shocked and then a little touched. "For me?"

"Of course we did," Artwhip said.

"Did you think we'd let you freeze to death or get eaten by snow-rooting fire-breathers?" Truman said.

"Well, don't get all mushy about it. You gave away all of our food, befuzzler!" he blustered. "What are we going to do now?"

"We could always change our minds and eat *you*," Otwell said.

"Very funny!" Coldwidder said.

They all laughed, just a little, but they kept their eyes peeled for the dezzles of fleet blinkers that might be lurking all around them.

CHAPTER TWENTY-SIX

Bound, Captured, Aloft

The path had disappeared. They were moving quickly through the forest, breathing hard. Plumes of steam rose from their mouths as if they were a train chugging up a mountain, Chickie leading the way. They leaned into the wind that would sometimes rip through the trees.

"Shouldn't we check the globes?" Truman asked.

"I'll look," Camille said, opening her backpack.

Artwhip passed the lantern back to Otwell, who walked behind the kids with the light poised over their heads.

Camille kept walking as she peered into the rounded glass. It showed a dark cave, filled with rows of glowing lights. "Flashlights?" she whispered. "No, not flashlights . . ." As the scene came more sharply into view, she saw that they were jars, not unlike Swelda's browsenberry wine jars. But these jars held lots of little blinking lights that moved around. The jars were filled with crawling bugs—lightning bugs. All kinds of strange creatures were carrying buckets and shovels and pickaxes. "It's a group of creatures all working underground like miners."

"What kinds of creatures?" Coldwidder asked.

"They're all different," Camille said, "except . . ." She squinted into the globe and saw dark chains clamped on their feet and paws and claws—all of them attached to the same row of chains. "They're all prisoners."

"That's where they were headed," Truman said. "Praddle and I saw a flock of caged creatures being carried up the mountain. And remember, Artwhip? In the alley outside of the ruckus tent?"

"That's right," Artwhip said. "A vulture, right there in the alley."

"Are they mining for something, or excavating?" Coldwidder asked.

"Dobbler had blueprints on his desk," Binderbee said. "He said he'd made a new alliance, one that would help with surveillance. It was with someone who might know where Cragmeal was and might know a thing or two about the Ever Breath."

Everyone was quiet for a moment. They were all thinking the same thing.

Camille finally said it aloud. "They're digging a new passageway."

"One that they can control—whoever they are," Artwhip said.

"And Dobbler is in on it," Binderbee said. "He wants to pin the robbery of the Ever Breath on Cragmeal, and put him away for good."

"And he'll team up with this new alliance of his, and then what?" Otwell asked.

"Everyone will be good, and evil will be done away with," Binderbee said.

"And what does that mean, exactly?" Camille asked.

"It means," Coldwidder said, "that Dobbler and this other person will be in total control of everything and everyone, and those who disagree, even in the slightest way, will be deemed unpatriotic betrayers and will be . . ."

"Done away with?" Truman asked. "Which means . . . ?"

"Killed," Otwell said.

Truman's stomach tightened to a knot. He looked at Camille, who'd gone pale.

"What about *your* globe, Truman?" Coldwidder asked urgently. "Maybe it will tell us something more."

Truman turned the globe over in his hands, and the snow in it swirled and kept swirling. He waited for it to settle, but it didn't. He stopped walking to keep the globe perfectly still, but the snow inside only seemed to whirl more violently. "It won't stop," he said. "It's like watching a snowstorm in a snow globe." And then he called to Otwell, "Lower the lantern! I need more light."

Otwell did as Truman had asked. "What is it?"

"It isn't snow," Truman said. "It's a swarm."

"Of what?" Camille asked.

But then suddenly, in the woods all around them, there was a flutter of white, what looked to be snow, except that it wasn't coming down from the sky. It was coming up from the ground.

"Locust fairies! Millions of them!" Coldwidder shouted.

"That's not all!" Artwhip shouted. "Dragonflies!"

One flew past Truman's ear. He saw that it wasn't the kind of dragonfly he knew. It was a tiny dragon—with a spiked tail, teeth, claws, and wings. On its back was a rider—a teeny, tiny man in a shiny red uniform and high black boots.

"Run!" Otwell bellowed.

"Run?" Camille said. "Away from fairies and dragonflies?"

"Trust us! Run!" Artwhip shouted.

Everyone started running then, but Truman had a hard time not being dazzled by the beauty of so many locust fairies—their spinning wings, the dart of their bodies through the night air, white wings rising up from the white ground, white lifting from white—and the darting swarm of dragonflies zipping among them. They poured through the trees. Truman felt like he was in a dream. He could feel fairy wings beating around his head, even lightly brushing his cheeks.

And then there were spiders, just like the ones he'd seen leaving town along the gutter that morning. They drifted down from the tree limbs on thin strands of silk and then they spun around Truman's body, twirling and twirling around him, as if he were a maypole.

Truman could hear his sister's voice off in the distance. "Where's Truman?" she shouted. "Truman!" And then he heard her shouting, "No! Get away!"

He heard a lot of voices then, all shouting at the same time—from Otwell's deep bass to Binderbee's squeak. But he couldn't see anything. His eyes were covered with webbing. His wrists were bound behind his back. And then the sea of tiny wings drifted off and a heavy set of wings descended. He felt a grip of claws pierce his jacket and then he was being pulled up from the earth, up and up and up.

CHAPTER TWENTY-SEVEN

Into the Dark Heart

And so Truman was up in the sky, cocooned in spiderwebs, his heart beating wildly in his chest.

The sound of the heavy, slow beating of the wings just above him and the taut feel of claws gripping the webbing at his back told him he was being transported by a vulture—a big one. Although he couldn't see, he could hear other wings beating around him. Was it a flock of vultures? Had locust fairies, spiders, and vultures captured all of them? Had they plucked Camille and Coldwidder from the ground? Had they snatched Artwhip right off of Chickie's back, as well as Otwell with Binderbee in his pocket?

Truman's mind started shifting from one thought to the next in rapid-fire images. He saw Swelda's parlor, the photograph of Ickbee and Swelda and their younger sister. He saw Ickbee's face, close up, the rolling pin frozen over her head, and then, in his mind's eye, his tiny view from the hollow log of the robe of locust fairies. He saw the museum again, with all of its strange and dusty items, and his father, as a little boy, being left there alone. There was Erswat in her hooded cloak, and the old music maker waving his four-fingered wave. The blood-betakers, the snow-rooting fire-breathers, the banshees, the swirling wings of locust fairies . . .

"C'mon, Truman," he muttered to himself. "Think!" He knew he needed help. He needed Camille. His mind flashed on the image of her in the window of Ickbee's hut, and the strange feeling of her voice in his ear even though she was miles away. Would it work if he tried it again? "Camille," he whispered, "are you there? Can you hear me?"

Everything was silent. He sighed.

But then he heard his name—a loud voice in his left ear, *Truman!*—and Camille's quick, choppy breaths. *I don't like this! Put me down!* she cried. And then she let out a scream.

Truman could hear the rush of water beneath him. They were following the path of a river, curving with each bend.

"Camille!" Truman called. "We've got to think!"

I'm not a survivor, Truman! Camille shouted. *I'm just me. I'm just a kid. I'm not tough at all. I just pretend to be. I miss home. I miss Mom even though she gets teary sometimes and goes all Jell-O, and I miss Dad—not the kid he is in this world, but our real grown-up dad who sings us that stupid song every night. I miss that stupid song!*

"It's okay, Camille. I'm just as scared as you are. But listen to me! Breathe! Just try to take deep breaths!"

There was silence—nothing but the sounds of the water below and the whipping air.

"Are you there?"

I'm breathing!

"Just pretend you're in a dream. A good dream where you get to fly. Haven't you ever flown in your dreams?"

No!

"Well, pretend anyway. It's a good dream."

It's a good dream. A good dream . . . very good dream . . .

"We've missed important clues," Truman said. "Little details that should tie everything together! I'm letting my mind go through all of the things we've experienced. We've got to rummage around and find some connection we've overlooked. Okay? Are you listening?"

Still breathing! Camille said.

Truman's bird dipped lower, gliding closer to the water. Truman could hear the rushing water under the bird's outstretched wings.

"The photograph," Truman said. He didn't know how much time was left. "The one of Swelda and Ickbee's little lost sister, Milta, with her scar, her jar of bugs. That locust-fairy robe I saw. Dad in the museum with the chopped-off finger in the glass case. The four-fingered wave of that music maker—"

Stop! Camille said.

"Are you talking to me or the vulture?" Truman said.

You, she said. *The chopped-off finger . . . did it belong to the music maker?* A roaring rush of water started to build. *Do you hear that?* she said.

"Block it out!" Truman pictured the chopped-off finger. "It was wearing a ring. A swirled design." His mind flashed back. "Milta had a scar, remember? A curlicue scar—the same shape as the ring's swirl!"

And then there was her jar of bugs—like the ones I saw in my globe lighting the passageway that the prisoners were digging! Camille said.

They seemed to be getting closer and closer to the rushing, roaring water. The only thing Truman could hear besides the water was Camille's voice, which seemed to come from within him.

Did Milta love bugs so much that she would make a robe out of them? Did she love them so much that she would give a locust-fairy fedora as a gift? "Could *she* be the one behind the locust fairies' stealing the Ever Breath?" Truman wondered aloud. "But isn't she long gone? Disappeared?"

And why, Camille said breathlessly, *why is she a sad story locked away in the family's sad sack?*

"And if she's the one behind it all, then who is T.T.S.?"

Truman's vulture gave a screeching call. Other vultures answered. The bird veered, swinging Truman's body outward and then back. The rushing water sounded even louder—a constant drumming in Truman's ears. He felt a misty spray, and then they seemed to be on the other side of it.

The air felt chilled and damp. There were strange cavelike echoes. The sound of the rushing water was still there, thrumming in the background.

Truman, Camille said. *Where are they taking us?*

"I don't know, but I feel we're getting closer to the Dark Heart, not farther away."

For a moment there were only the strange echoes and the noise of rushing water. And then Truman heard Camille's voice again in his ear. *Truman?*

"Yes?"

You were right.

And Truman didn't have to ask her what he was right about. He knew what she meant. This place did belong to them and they belonged to it. "Thanks," Truman whispered, and he hoped that she knew what he meant: Thanks for saying that, but also thanks for everything. Mainly, thanks for being his sister even though she didn't have much of a choice.

CHAPTER TWENTY-EIGHT

T.T.S.

The vulture set Truman down and with one quick snap of its beak snipped the webbing that covered his eyes. His wrists were still bound behind his back. There he stood, facing a wooden door that was engraved with a large swirl right in its center. In the middle of the swirl there was a peephole, and on the other side of the peephole was one large blue eye, blinking at him. The peephole was not at adult height. It was right at Truman's level.

"Hello?" Truman said.

The eye disappeared.

And then Truman heard a deep bellow behind him.

He turned around and saw an enormous cave with a waterfall pouring down over the center of its opening. Rushing in around the waterfall on either side were more vultures. They were carrying Coldwidder, Artwhip, and Camille. And then there were three vultures hauling in Otwell—one clamped to the back of his shirt and two holding up his legs. He was the source of the bellowing.

"Easy now! Not upside down, please! I've got a mouse hanging on for dear life!"

There was Binderbee hanging on to the edge of Otwell's breast pocket—wide-eyed with fear, the wind rippling his fur.

One by one, the vultures dropped their captives in front of the door.

"See! I told you I'd get you to the Dark Heart!" Coldwidder said.

"Thanks a lot!" Binderbee said. "I almost fell to my death!" He was severely windblown; his fur had been gusted in every direction.

"I don't feel so good," Camille said, looking blanched.

Truman thought of the foggy, twisting roads that his mother had driven over to get to their grandmother's house. And, oddly enough, as nervous as he felt, he didn't feel the least bit queasy. "Carsick?"

"No, vulture-sick!"

The vulture who'd carried Truman squawked, ruffled its wings, walked up to the door, and knocked with its beak.

"Bring them in!" The voice was high-pitched and giddy, as if they were the first guests to show up at a birthday party.

The door opened and there stood the music maker. He smiled and waved his signature four-fingered wave, and then his eyes landed on Artwhip. "You!" he said. "I told you to play dead! Well, it's not my fault if you're going to have go through it all over again. I'll make sure I get it right this time!"

"Good luck with that," Artwhip muttered.

The vultures shoved everyone into the room, their hands bound behind their backs, and slammed the door, standing guard. The room was pulsing with white wings, so much so that it was almost impossible to see. Through little glimpses, though, Truman recognized this as the overstuffed room he'd seen in the globe, the one that looked like a museum. The locust-fairy wings were a constant buzz, but there were also distant noises—tromping, banging, clatter, and thuds—coming from somewhere deeper in the Dark Heart.

"This is it!" Truman said.

Through the beating wings, he glimpsed the taxidermied creatures frozen in moments of terror or pain, and the enormous collection of weaponry mounted on the walls, which were draped in velvet. Truman searched for his father, but to no avail.

Finally there was a sharp whistle, and the white flutter of wings swarmed around a small shape that walked out from behind an enormous stuffed reindeerlike creature. The locust fairies quickly fluttered to form a cloak around the figure. All Truman could see were small black boots.

It was the creature he'd seen while lying in the hollow log with Praddle.

This person was about Truman and Camille's size, and moved in a bouncy young way. But a large lump sat on the figure's curled shoulders.

"Who are you?" Artwhip asked.

"Let's play a guessing game!" The voice that rose up from the cloak was girlish. "I'm not the first sister and I'm not the second sister."

"You're the third sister?" Camille said.

"Yes!" the voice said. "Isn't that enough of a clue?"

Truman thought for a moment. "The third sister. T.T.S.?"

"Oooooh! You're good at games!" She then turned to face

all of them and very slowly lowered her hood. And there was Milta, with her blond hair and her curlicue scar. She was still a little girl, young in every way, except the hump on her back.

"You're a forever child too," Truman said.

"Did my hateful sisters forget to mention that? They've always enjoyed forgetting me! Like the time they forgot to pick me up from my evil music teacher's house on the day that the man struck me across the cheek for not practicing and I got this awful scar!"

The music maker stepped forward. "I had problems with my temper back then, but she cured me of that!"

"As soon as I ran away from home, I hunted him down and chopped off the finger with the ring—fully intact!" She pointed to the glass jar sitting on a high shelf. "Ring and all! Quite beautiful now!"

The music maker rubbed the nub on his hand and glowered.

"I'd love to chop him to bits completely, but he's so loyal!" She smiled at the music maker sweetly. "I like to collect. Mostly objects of suffering, but I'll also collect sorrow, despair, agony!"

Camille spoke up. "Didn't you have a snow globe—a gift from your father? There is a third one. Isn't there?"

"No," Milta said quickly. "I smashed it!" She turned on her heel and took a few marching steps. "That doesn't matter now. None of it does! Anyway, I've been awaiting an audience! Let me give you a behind-the-scenes look at the new exhibit that I'm planning to unveil!"

She clapped and a few locust fairies flew over to a velvet

curtain that hid one corner of the room. They lifted the curtain and tied it back, revealing a boy in a gilded cage.

"Camille! Truman!" the boy said.

It was their father—a kid in a tall, narrow cage, his hands gripping the bars, his face dusty and thin. On the wall behind his cage was the wrought-iron key on a hook.

"Being a forever child runs in the family!" Milta said.

Truman and Camille started to run to him, but Milta's voice stopped them in their tracks. "Please stay on this side of the velvet rope!"

They froze.

"Listen to her very carefully," their father said. He looked up at the top of the cage. Some fat spiders were creeping along the upper bars, and there, suspended over their father's head from the ceiling of the cage was an orb—an amber orb with a wavering glow within it.

The breath of A Being Than Which Nothing Greater Can Be Conceived embedded in a stone!

The Ever Breath.

"Holy, holy!" Otwell cried.

Coldwidder gasped and sank to his knees.

Artwhip said, "It's still breathing! See, Truman, anything is possible. It's alive."

Truman could barely breathe himself. "That's really it," Camille whispered. "Isn't it?"

"It has to be," Truman said.

But as they looked more closely at the orb, they could see that it was suspended by the fine silken webbing, and strands were connected to their father's arms and legs. He couldn't move or the Ever Breath itself might fall and smash.

"I set up this system, with a bit of spider power, because I didn't want him to try to slip away," Milta told them. "He can be very clever, you know—but not as clever as I am!" The locust fairies of her robe quivered in agreement.

"What are you going to do with him?" Truman asked, his mind whirling. Milta was crazy.

"Ah, well, I have the Ever Breath. My sisters seem to think I'm too little to know how to do anything! But, see, I've been spending my life preparing for this, hidden away under this cloak of locust fairies so that they can never see my face, even through their blasted seeing globes. I've lived among the blood-betakers and werefolk, learning a certain necessary comfort with hunting to the death. It came to me surprisingly naturally." She pointed to a taxidermied blood-betaker wearing a medallion, and a snarling wolven man. "I killed and stuffed some of their lesser royalty as souvenirs. And I've learned from the banshees how to have power over animals." She showcased a few snow-rooting fire-breathers. "And I have a special bond with insects. I always have.

"And, of course, I've enjoyed weaponry and also I've had a lot of fun!" She whirled around the room, and her hump-back looked very much out of place, since everything else about her was spry and light. She stopped at a wall-mounted unicorn's head. "The unicorn!" She winked. "And, oh! The reindeer, for example—oh so slightly human in the face, this species is! How I enjoy shooting them with automatic arrows from atop my vulture! They never expect an attack by air!"

In one corner, there was a small horned man wearing an

Edwell's Hops and Chops House apron and bow tie. "What about him?" Coldwidder asked.

"Him?" She looked at the waiter with her head tilted as if she couldn't quite remember. Then she snapped her fingers. "Oh, that's right! Cold soup! I was irritated, so I had him stuffed."

"Oh."

"Now, if you put it all together—A, my frustration at being the littlest, most forgotten, and overlooked child in my family, the one who was *not* a twin and therefore *not* entrusted with guarding the passageway in either direction, and B, my love of killing and stuffing things—that will lead you to C: I want my own passageway because I deserve it! And while I'm having it dug for me, why not create my very own pedestal for the Ever Breath?"

"What do you mean?" Truman asked, trying to twist his hands against the webbing on his wrists.

"That old tree root of a hand! Ha! That will never do. Not for me! I'm going to use"—she turned to their father—"I'm going to use your father here! I'll have him stuffed in the perfect pose so it's our very own Cragmeal, Dead King of the Jarkmen, holding the Ever Breath in the new passageway for *me* forever! What better way to commemorate a new reign?"

"But I thought it took two people to replace the Ever Breath, one on either side," Camille said. "If you don't get it right, both worlds will die!"

"And then don't you need two people to guard the passageway?" Truman added. "Twins?"

Milta squeezed her eyes shut and slammed her hands over

her ears. "I WILL NOT HEAR OF TWINS! I WILL NOT HEAR OF TWINS! I WILL NOT HEAR OF TWINS!" She opened her eyes and looked around.

No one said a word.

"See, I *have* another person," Milta said. "I've struck a deal." She clapped and a few locust fairies flew to another velvety drape and pulled it back, then tied it with golden ropes. There was an arched opening painted gold. The sounds of banging and chipping and thumping got louder. This was Milta's passageway.

She walked up to it and shouted: "Wilward!"

"Coming!" And in a few seconds, Truman saw the feathered man from all of the US VERSUS THEM! posters.

"Dobbler!" Binderbee said. "I knew it."

He strode in holding rolled blueprints under his arm and wearing the locust-fairy fedora. "Hidy ho!" he said, very chipper. "I see the vultures have brought more prisoners! Well, there isn't much more to do! We're making great progress. Almost done. But I'll find something—"

"Wilward!" Milta interrupted. "These aren't more prisoners that you can set to work. These are my captives! The ones who think they're going to take back the Ever Breath and free Cragmeal."

"Oh!" he said, and then his eyes fell on Binderbee. "Wait, you! You're supposed to be on *our* side! Us versus Them!"

"And what are you doing here with the enemy?" Binderbee shouted. "Us versus *who?*"

"Don't you criticize me! This is a means to an end. Sometimes you have to do bad things to make good things happen!"

"You use fear to hold people hostage, to get more power

just like the enemy." Binderbee strained against the webs that held back his small arms. "But you do it to your own people. You trick them, which makes you even worse than the enemy!"

Dobbler turned to Milta. "You talked me into having Cragmeal stuffed. Why not stuff the rest of them too so he won't be lonesome?"

"Always thinking of others, Dobbler. That's what makes you so admirable!"

Binderbee backed away, hiding behind Otwell's boots.

There was some busy talk then—Milta and Dobbler trying to decide just how to kill them. He preferred something quick. The construction was coming along swiftly and he didn't want to waste time. She preferred something a little more creative. "A devilish kind of contraption that chops them up!"

"If they're chopped up," the music maker interrupted, "then it'll be hard to stuff them. So much stitching!"

Truman wasn't sure exactly when Binderbee stiffened his tail and used it to pick apart the webbing on himself, but the mouse was quick. He scurried up Otwell's pant leg first, nibbling through the webbing with his sharp teeth, and then he moved on down the line until they were all standing there, completely still, as if their wrists were still tied, when in fact they weren't.

The only problem of course was Truman and Camille's father. If they started a fight, he might get jostled, and even the slightest shift could dislodge the Ever Breath, sending it to the floor of the cage, where it would shatter.

But they also knew that they didn't have much time. The

pedestal hand in the passageway at Ickbee's house—it had to be closing, quickly.

They all exchanged nervous glances. *What now?*

At that moment, Truman noticed one of the spiders. It was a large, hairy spider, much like the others. But this one seemed angrier, more determined. He was moving quickly from spider to spider, whispering something. Soon, all of the spiders were moving—silently but swiftly—as Milta and Dobbler were fighting about efficiency and creativity and power and the art of living.

"This isn't just some stupid hobby of mine, you know," Milta was saying. "I'm not a little kid! I'm an artist! This is my art!"

"We've got a job to do," Dobbler countered. "Once you have real power, you can create all the deathly art you want."

Some of the spiders were detaching the webs from Cragmeal while others were reinforcing the webbing around the Ever Breath—so much so that it disappeared in a white cocoon.

And when they were done, the spider leader seemed to give Truman a nod.

And then the sign came.

With Binderbee secure in his breast pocket, Otwell Prim, the Ogre of the Webbly Wood, grabbed his sword, swung it over his head, and let out an enormous whoop.

CHAPTER TWENTY-NINE

Battle in the Dark Heart

Coldwidder and Artwhip had their daggers out in no time. The vultures were upon them with talons and beaks. There were glinting blades and quick-swiping claws.

Otwell was spinning and turning—a dervish with a sword. Binderbee burrowed down in his pocket, where he could hear the ogre's heart pounding in his chest. A few times Binderbee peeked out to see the sword swishing on this side and then the other. There were three vultures attacking Otwell at the same time. But he kept pivoting. Feathers were flitting through the air madly.

Dobbler hid behind the stuffed reindeer, but Milta ran to the wall of weapons and grabbed a long, thin sword. She laughed and spun around the room. "Oh, impromptu art! This is such a whimsical kind of killing! I'd like to start with the children!"

The music maker wrung his hands and skittered behind one of the velvet curtains. "Be careful!" he cried. "No one can hurt Milta! That is the rule!"

Truman and Camille ran to the wall too, grabbing

swords to protect themselves. Milta was so quick and agile, even under the weight of her hump, that they were both struggling to block her quick jabs. The locust fairies were dithering nervously all around her, their wings making her sound electrified.

Truman and Camille dodged behind the stuffed blood-betaker and the wolven man.

"Help!" Dobbler screamed into the passageway. "Help us! We're being attacked!"

In the distance could be heard heavy footfalls, the clinking of chains. The footfalls grew louder and louder and then the room was filled with prisoners. There were wolves and horned men and horse-heads and snake-heads and glowskins and urfs and weaselwomen—every kind of creature you can imagine—chained together and covered in dirt.

Their warden was standing there, looking nervous and shaken. "Sir," he said, "are you sure that this is wise?"

"I order all of you to protect us from these evildoers! If you do, I'll set you all free!" Dobbler screamed. He was gripping the stuffed reindeer's fur and crying. "It's Us versus Them!"

Everyone froze.

A wolf stood up on his hind legs, walked over to the wall, pulled off a double-sided sword, and passed it down the chain. "Us versus who?" he asked. And he pulled off more weapons and passed them down.

"Us versus Them!" Dobbler cried.

In the meantime, Cragmeal had been quietly working. He'd gotten the key off the hook by fishing with his belt, had inched his fingers to it, pinched it, and pulled it into the cage, and now he unlocked the cage door. He reached up and pulled the cocooned Ever Breath from the ceiling of his cage and stepped into the room.

"We don't believe in *us* and *them*," Cragmeal said. "We're jarkmen."

And with that, Milta screamed, "No! It's mine!" With all of her might, she ran and leapt through the air, her sword held firm. The locust fairies went fluttering off behind her like billowing smoke, and when Cragmeal dodged her, she went flying. She landed, took a few jerky steps, and then ran into the horn of the unicorn, which pierced the meat of her shoulder and sent her falling backward onto the floor. And . . .

There lay a little girl in a red dress with a long, thin sword in her hand. There was no hump at all—only a sack. An old tattered sack. It had come loose and its contents were spilled across the floor.

There were two photographs—one of each of her sisters— an old jar with holes poked in its rusty lid, and a snow globe. She hadn't smashed it after all. She'd carried it with her all these years.

"Her sad sack," Camille said.

Dobbler hid his head in his hands and cried.

Everyone else gathered around Milta, worrying whether she was alive or dead.

The music maker appeared from behind the curtain. "Milta!" he cried, and he ran to her side and gathered all of her things and put them back in her sack. "No," he said, "you can't see her like this! No!"

He grabbed the long, thin sword. "Back up," he said. "Get away!"

Everyone shuffled backward, and then he whistled through his teeth and the locust fairies covered her in a cloak and also lifted her up, as if on a fluttering white cloud, and carried her to the unfinished passageway, the one that likely led nowhere.

"It's okay, my girl," he said. "It's okay!"

CHAPTER THIRTY

Riding the Fire-Breather

Truman and Camille followed their father out of the room, into the echoey cave. He had the Ever Breath clutched to his heart. Artwhip, Coldwidder, Otwell, and Binderbee were on their heels. All of them were still fighting off the vultures that were dive-bombing them with their talons and beaks.

But mainly the vultures had to contend with the prisoners, who were free now. The warden had let them all loose. He'd had no choice. He and Dobbler had already been shoved into Cragmeal's cage for safekeeping.

"We've got to get Truman and Camille back down the mountain fast!" their father shouted.

"But how?" Truman said.

They came to a skidding stop at the edge of the cave— the waterfall pouring down from overhead in front of them and the white rapids below.

Artwhip shook his head. "We need some help," he said.

Just then a cloud of smoke rose up around them and there, fluttering up from the mist, was Chickie—her wings unfurled and flapping wildly.

"You can fly!" Otwell cried.

She heaved herself onto the moist ledge to the right of the falls.

"Okay, then," their father said. "You two have to go. She can't take any more weight than that." He grabbed them and the three children embraced. "I'm sorry," he whispered. "I should have figured out a way so you wouldn't have had to—"

"It's okay," Camille said.

"We understand now," Truman said.

And with that they climbed on Chickie's back, Truman holding tight to the amber orb.

"Oh," Camille said, "one more thing. The best way to survive jumping off a waterfall. Hands locked over your head. Jump far enough out to avoid the rocks and start swimming hard right away, downstream."

"And call for Erswat!" Truman said. "Once you're in the water, call her name."

"Erswat!" Artwhip said. "Of course!"

Camille held the reins and Truman held the Ever Breath, and with a frantic effort, Chickie flapped her wings and they took off in a sputtery motion.

Chickie huffed and smoked and let out noxious fumes, but she was drifting in the right direction, heading downhill.

"Oh no!" Camille cried. "I'll never get used to flying like this!"

"Distract yourself," Truman said. "And don't close your eyes. It only makes it worse."

From this perch, Truman and Camille could see the snowy fields, the forest paths, the river, and the bog.

And soon enough they saw a tiny caved-in hut of brittle, broken mud and broken vines. Chickie alighted in the front yard and then collapsed.

"You did good!" Truman shouted, holding tight to the Ever Breath.

Camille put her hands on her knees for a second, regaining her strength. And then they both ran to the door, which had snapped in two under the strain of the house and left a gaping hole. They crawled inside and found that they had to keep crawling. The roof had nearly completely caved in. The air was dusty and dry, which made Camille cough. "I'm allergic to everything here!"

There were a few mewlers still roaming.

"Praddle?" Truman called.

Then he heard her voice. "Thisss way," she hissed.

They crawled toward her voice and found her standing beside the small passageway.

"Where is Ickbee?" Camille asked.

"She'sss waiting for you."

"In there?" Truman asked.

Praddle nodded.

And so Camille and Truman crawled down the passageway, Praddle following them. The passageway was narrow and shriveled—so tight they had to drag and dig and pull themselves along. Finally they saw a bit of light, and then they saw the room. It had shrunk so much that the hand itself was scraping the ceiling. It was almost completely curled into a fist—the only thing that remained was the smallest bit of air between the thumb curling over, about to lock it shut forever.

And there on either side of the hand were Ickbee and

Swelda, two old women in their wooly blue hats, holding the ceiling up with their bare hands. They were shaking. "Hurry," they said in unison.

Truman held up the Ever Breath.

"There's an important question to ask before you take this final step," Swelda said. "Who will live in the Breath World and who will live in the Fixed? Do you know?"

Truman and Camille looked at each other and nodded.

Praddle paced between them.

"Whoever will live in the Fixed World needs to hold the Ever Breath with one hand on this side of the passageway," Swelda said.

"And the one who'll live in the Breath World will stand with me on the other," Ickbee said.

Camille walked over to Swelda, and Truman stood by Ickbee, with Praddle nearby.

Each holding up one side of the orb, the twins lifted the Ever Breath and touched it to the thumb.

The hand quivered, then shook, and finally bloomed open, and the Ever Breath slipped back into its fingers.

The roots, all around them, rippled and then tightened like muscles, and the ceiling and walls were pulled back into place.

Truman and Camille stepped away, each on his or her side of the Ever Breath. Truman picked up Praddle.

"We did it," Truman said.

"We did," Camille said.

Ickbee grinned and Swelda wiped tears from her cheeks.

Camille pulled off her backpack and took out the two snow globes. She handed one to Truman.

Camille shook hers first. The snow globe showed Artwhip, Coldwidder, Otwell, and Binderbee being rescued from rapids and guided toward shore by a group of strong, lean bogpeople. Erswat was there, too, helping Artwhip keep his head above the churning water. Truman and Camille's father had already made it to the muddy bank. He was wet and looked cold and shivery, but his mouth was shaped in a perfect O—as if, at that very moment, he was singing at the top of his lungs.

Truman shook his next. The snow swirled up and finally settled—on a face. A girl with blond curls and a curlicue scar on her cheek. She seemed to be asleep or worse—dead.

"Milta!" Swelda said.

Ickbee gasped and then gave a sad sigh.

The girl's eyes fluttered open, and for a moment she looked surprised, almost happy. But then her face tightened into an angry, vengeful glare.

Milta was very much alive.

JULIANNA BAGGOTT

lives with her family in Florida. She is the author of many wonderful books for children and adults, including the Anybodies trilogy, written under the name N. E. Bode, which *People* magazine described as "Potter-style magic meets Snicket-y irreverence," and *The Prince of Fenway Park*.

As a child, she always had an inkling that snow globes could reveal other worlds, if they wanted to. And now she knows the truth!

YEARLING FANTASY!

Looking for more great fantasy books to read? Check these out!

- ❏ *Any Which Wall* by Laurel Snyder
- ❏ *Earth's Magic* by Pamela F. Service
- ❏ *First Light* by Rebecca Stead
- ❏ *Gossamer* by Lois Lowry
- ❏ *The Princess and the Unicorn* by Carol Hughes

TRY A TRILOGY!

BOOKS OF EMBER
by Jeanne DuPrau

- ❏ *The City of Ember*
- ❏ *The People of Sparks*
- ❏ *The Diamond of Darkhold*

THE INDIAN IN THE CUPBOARD
by Lynne Reid Banks

- ❏ *The Indian in the Cupboard*
- ❏ *The Return of the Indian*
- ❏ *The Secret of the Indian*

HIS DARK MATERIALS
by Philip Pullman

- ❏ *The Golden Compass*
- ❏ *The Subtle Knife*
- ❏ *The Amber Spyglass*

MY FATHER'S DRAGON
by Ruth Stiles Gannett

- ❏ *My Father's Dragon*
- ❏ *Elmer and the Dragon*
- ❏ *The Dragons of Blueland*

Visit **www.randomhouse.com/kids** for additional reading suggestions in adventure, mystery, humor, and nonfiction!